Extreme Prejudice

Imogene's Message

Christine Sherborne

Extreme Prejudice

Imogene's Message

Copyright 2014 by Christine Sherborne

Published by Colourstory Pty Ltd

Cover Image by Hugh Sherborne

ISBN 978-1-921501-22-7

Print Edition

I dedicate this novel to Don McNair, editor extraordinaire.

Don edited this book, mentored me, and taught me to write.

Thank you Don, your legacy lives on in the many people you have helped.

TABLE OF CONTENTS

CHAPTER ONE

Was that them coming back?

Xantara Pembroke trembled as she held her breath, listening to the sounds from the church sanctuary above. No, it was the rats. It had to be the rats. Now she heard them in the crypt outside her cell.

She flinched as their claws again broke the stillness, now scratching against the cold stone flags. Rats! Her heart pounded as she clasped her hands across her chest to calm herself. She took several deep breaths to stave off a panic attack, to become grounded.

Darkness surrounded her like a thick icy mantle, relieved by a single shaft of watery light that fought its way through an iron grid high above her. She drew a threadbare, mildewed blanket closer around her slender frame and hunched over. She rocked, small movements, back and forth.

Her light cotton dress didn't stop the cold from the hard stone seeping into her bones. She wrinkled her nose at the musty odor of black earth mixed with decay from a heap of discarded religious paraphernalia. Her skin felt clammy, whether from fear or the damp, she didn't know.

Is this some sort sick joke?

The faint light grew stronger as the moon climbed into the night sky. It streamed through the cell bars, then reflected up from her white summer sandals. A pile of dusty hymn books balanced precariously on discarded oaken pews. As she'd guessed, she sat in the crypt of St Michael's.

The old Norman church perched high on a craggy outcrop surrounded by dark, empty fields. Faded paintings of Norman soldiers decorated the wall opposite, and the three cells, fitted with iron bars, stored communion wine and other church artifacts. One cell was packed with furniture and old church vestments.

She realized no one would hear her shouts, so she sat, a pale presence, waiting in silence. A candle stub and box of matches lay on a three-legged stool next to her. Her hands shook as she struck a match. The flame flickered, then sprang into life as the smell of sulfur surrounded her. She huddled over the flame, but drew little comfort from its warmth. The glow highlighted tendrils of pure white hair which flowed over her shoulders, and the darkness accentuated the pearlescent albino skin on her bare arms, which resembled the surface of a cold marble statue.

A time-worn, plastic-lined milking pail had been left for her convenience. In pain, she struggled across the uneven stone floor and relieved herself. Tired and bruised after her failed struggle, her arms throbbed. She rubbed them, and the pain lessened. She sank onto a narrow cot and dropped her head into her hands. A sigh of despair escaped her lips.

She clenched her fists. How could she have been so damned stupid? She shouldn't have trusted them! Why did she ignore her gut feeling? Why on earth did she agree? Her outburst bounced around the vault, its echo diminishing as it lost power. She should have realized. What a bunch of fanatics!

Her shoulders slumped as she reflected on events that led up to her imprisonment. It was obvious in hindsight. They used surveillance, watched her every move, perhaps even witnessed a ceremony. She hoped not.

Her actions were misconstrued, twisted by warped minds, their real significance lost. They didn't understand, but judged her, anyway. Prejudice and bigotry radiated from them, a foul stench so palpable she imagined black, misty auras curling around each evil one of them. She felt blood pounding through a vein in her neck, felt her face flush.

Her sixth sense warned her off, but Braeden hurt so much. It seemed such an innocent request. After all, what damage could a harmless church group do?

She stretched out in an attempt to get comfortable. As she lay back, she heard a ragged cry.

"Who's there?"

A weak, hoarse voice answered. "Xantara, is that you?"

"Yes, who is it?"

"Jonathan."

She knew the young man at once. He'd arrived in the village not long after she, Braeden, and their seven year old daughter Imogene did eleven months before, and opened a hairdressing salon just two doors down from the clinic where her husband was the physician and she worked as a nurse and midwife. She pictured him, tall and thin, his tangle of ginger hair atop a face covered with typical teenage spots which stood out like a rough moonscape against his sun-reddened skin. She liked him right away. His ready smile showing his perfect white teeth flashed often, made her day feel brighter. She found him helpful and pleasant, and an excellent hairdresser.

"Why are you here?" she asked. "Are you all right?"

"No! They mangled my hand!" Another muffled sob escaped his lips. "How can I do hair now? They'll be back soon."

She ran her fingers through her hair, then let it fall back. "They've hurt you? I can't believe it."

"They pushed my fingers into a metal bone crusher, one at a time." He moaned, apparently remembering the painful agony.

Blood pounded in her ears. "Who did this?"

"I don't know. I was sweeping the floor, when someone pulled a sack over my head and held a smelly cloth over my face. Then I woke up here." He yelled into the darkness. "What have I done? Please, let me out!"

She immediately knew his "crime." It stood out like a circus in town.

It was obviously the same group who'd dragged her down here, her head also covered with a sack. Why the sack? Of course. Intimidation, shock tactics, their tools of choice. But he's just a boy, how could they?

The lad quieted, and she thought about events that had led up to their predicament. The church group was behind it.

The group met on Thursday nights, right there, upstairs. She refused to go, but Braeden attended every meeting. A few villagers knew the group's radical views, and sometimes let details slip. As a midwife and nurse she tended many locals, and heard plenty. She was shocked by the outrageous tales, and dismissed them. Big mistake!

She turned her attention back to the boy. How could she reassure him?

"Take a breath," she said, "and calm down. I'm sure they're just out to scare you." She herself took a deep breath, determined to sound upbeat, although she knew she was lying. "They'll let you go. After all, what else can they do?"

The boy cried louder. Her stomach contracted with concern as he wept in despair. What can we do?

"They" were a splinter group affiliated with St Michael's church. Some of the rumors called them a zealous Fundamentalist sect, others thought them more sinister. Intolerant to "sinners," some said. They wanted to cleanse the area of practices they considered abhorrent. Apparently, their targets were anyone outside their group. Now they'd put their plans into action by kidnapping Jonathan and her.

The young man cried out for his Mum. His voice became childish as he grew more fearful.

"It'll be all right," she whispered. "We'll tell the police as soon as we get out. Then we'll take you to hospital and get your hand fixed."

She leaned back against the stone wall, thinking. They wouldn't go any further, would they? She knew why she was chosen. She shivered as her imagination ran wild. What would they do to her, if they could mutilate a young man like Jonathan? She drew her knees to her chest and clutched the star that dangled from its silver chain.

They must have singled her out when the village clinic re-opened. Then, her unusual name gave her away. Xantara, meant "protector of the earth," an ancient name passed down through the centuries, its source lost in antiquity. She carried on a sacred tradition, privileged to bear the honored title.

Her thoughts wandered. So much had happened since they moved to the village.

Her daughter Imogene wriggled about, peering over the front car seat. Her face beamed as they approached Monkton St Michael and drove down the High Street. Braeden would start his new job soon, as the village doctor. For the last few years, he'd worked as an emergency physician in Swindon, but she'd always known he preferred the variety and friendliness of a small village. And now they were here.

"This is it." He stopped the car in front of the clinic. Xantara and Imogene jumped out as he searched the glove box for the key, then opened the front door. They stepped in.

The well-ordered waiting room had a dozen chairs placed against the walls, and a coffee table held a collection of tatty, out-of-date magazines. The doctor's office looked comfortable. A padded but worn chair sat in front of a wide modern desk. Pictures of muscles and skeletons hung next to an eye chart on the wall.

They entered the living quarters, accessed from the office. She saw the terraced house ran from front to back, one room wide but five rooms in length. It charmed her from the start.

Together, they explored. Imogene skipped from room to room, chattering away as she swung her arms. They walked through the cottage and Xantara admired the compact rooms. She discovered the stairs, out of sight behind the kitchen, and climbed the worn wooden steps to inspect the three small bedrooms and single bathroom. Imogene followed her, then ran ahead. The front bedroom's window overlooked the street. "I want this one, Mummy."

Together they went back down and inspected the renovated extension. It would make a brilliant sunroom, she realized, an ideal place to relax with a good book. The forty-five feet long back garden included a vegetable patch filled with cabbages and beans. A small orchard consisted of three trees; a pear, an apple and a plum. She crossed her arms and smiled at the scene. The whole house and business was perfect! The whitewashed walls would set off their dark furniture a treat.

Xantara's best friend Bryony arrived as arranged with a housewarming gift, a bowl planted with flowering pink hyacinths. Both were born and bred in nearby Avebury, only twenty minutes away, and it had been hard for them when Xantara moved to Swindon. Now they could see more of each other.

The childhood friends hugged, and Xantara led Bryony into the kitchen. "Let's enjoy some fresh lemonade on the veranda," she said, opening the clinic fridge. "Braeden, will you oversee the movers while we catch up? Remember that big box labeled "miscellaneous" goes into the kitchen."

She poured and they went to the shady veranda, and they were soon laughing and sharing anecdotes about their fun-filled childhood days when they chased each other around Avebury Circle. The monolithic stones were just a normal part of their young world, but now Xantara realized the powerful historic site was a central part of their lives. The three thousand year old stone circle held a power that nearby Stonehenge had lost centuries ago. It predated the more famous site by nearly a thousand years.

She sipped the last of her lemonade and sat the sweat-covered glass onto the little glass-topped table. Well, let's explore the village," she said, jumping up. She went to the door. "Imogene, want to come along?"

Within moments they were walking arm in arm toward the lake, with Imogene running ahead, then lagging behind as she explored odd-shaped rocks and hopping frogs. She wedged between them and grabbed their hands, and soon they were swinging her high between them.

As they talked, Xantara glanced about at her new surroundings. The Wiltshire Downs area had many villages similar to Monkton St Michael, but none as isolated. She studied the quaint cottages made from local sandstone, many with thatched roofs. The cobbled main street added to its charm.

They stopped at the lake edge and sat on a council bench. The lake looked dark, mystical even, its surface hidden under a rolling blanket of mist. Xantara squinted as she peered over the strange water. The thick haze blurred details of the small island in the centre, and she could barely make out the shape of an ancient stone ruin, black against the sky.

Bryony saw her staring, and followed her gaze toward the island. "What is that?" she asked, pointing.

"It's just a ruin," Xantara said. "The locals call it 'The Isle of Angels' after the Archangel St Michael. They've made the island a bird sanctuary. The road ends at the lake, so no one ventures off the main highway, except for the wildlife, of course."

As they watched Imogene wade in the gentle ripples of waves that lapped over the smooth stones, Xantara thought of her son Alistair. Since he lived on campus at Cambridge University and was busy with lectures, he hadn't been able to help with the move.

What a beautiful day. We should treasure such days as they never return.

Distant metallic sounds echoed off the church basement walls, and the scrape of a door jolted Xantara back to the present. She clutched herself tighter, as relentless memories of the moving day flooded her mind. The mysterious island metamorphosed into a monster's lair. The dark ruin had changed her life in a heartbeat, leaving grief and destruction behind. As she remembered that terrible day, a black despair settled over her, and she began to shake.

Fremont Braxton, holding a paraffin lamp, clattered down the stone steps. Xantara had first seen him on moving day, when she visited his butcher shop for sandwich meat to hold them until they could shop properly. He'd bowed and grinned, and asked her if she'd ever tried spiced luncheon meat. Now, as he waved the lantern back and forth inspecting her and her fellow prisoner, the light revealed a cold frown on his coarse, florid-complexioned face. His vast stomach swelled over his belt under a clean, white butcher's apron, the result of too many large meat and potato dinners.

Next Eamon and Gloria Tierney came into view, an elfin Irish couple who looked so innocent. Behind them was her worst nightmare, Ezekiel Yates, the pack leader, with his dutiful wife Millicent at his side. The group's final duo, Archie and Ethel Redford, brought up the rear, looking like simple country folk, almost yokels. In a different time and place they'd be wearing rough country smocks and have strands of straw sticking out of their mouths.

How could they be involved? They'd been so kind after the accident. The meals, the visits… they couldn't do enough for her this past week. Ethel avoided her gaze and looked at Archie, as he looked back at her. Their shame radiated across the room.

As the seven stood in silence, Eamon inserted four rush torches into eye-level wall sconces. Xantara shank back as far as possible from the bars and saw Jonathan do the same, his face ashen. As Eamon approached, the torches' flames sprang up and danced on the walls. The eerie light flickered over the ghoulish group, their faces taking on a sinister luminosity.

Xantara heard another set of steps, and turned to peer behind them. It was her husband! She drew in a sharp breath and her hands flew to her chest.

"Braeden! What are you doing here?"

He didn't answer. The flames emphasized his shock of blonde hair and his Germanic blue eyes which, hard as diamonds, avoided hers. He looked at the floor, then away.

She glared at him. Unbelievable. How could he accept all this? Why doesn't he stop this bizarre charade? He'd stood by and let them take her without saying a word.

Their marriage had strengthened as each year passed. Even the accident drew them closer. Could it fall apart now? She'd supported him without reservation for twenty-three years, working two jobs while he earned his doctor's degree for the last seven. Now he'd betrayed her.

Torn up with grief after the accident, he'd accepted the group's sympathetic support. Who could have known they would brainwash him? She realized only now that he'd been taken in by their radical views. A sudden coldness prickled her scalp, her eyes squeezed shut.

She understood his search for answers, some reason and understanding in the situation. The accident had changed everything. His atheism no longer served him. There was no hope for him, and he needed to believe in something, a future. Now she realized his vulnerable state had made him ripe for the plucking.

"Braeden, help me. Please."

He didn't respond. His blank stare now focused on something above her head. Her shoulders stiffened. She wouldn't ask again. She concentrated on his eyes, trying to fathom the thoughts behind them.

Ezekiel Yates motioned to two men, and they unlocked the door of the neighboring cell with a massive iron key. Jonathan struggled and kicked as they dragged him out.

A coarse, altar-like flat stone lay in the crypt's center, a rusted iron ring hanging down on each side. They pushed him face down onto the stone, shackled his hands to the rings, and bared his back. He screamed in pain as the chains rubbed against his crushed fingers. His breathing was ragged as he sucked in air. Horrified, she stared.

What on earth would they do next? It's the twenty-first century, for goodness sake!

Ezekiel, beads of sweat on his forehead, flashed a cold smile and opened his bible. He began reading a passage, in a deep bass voice that filled the room.

"Do not be deceived: neither the sexually immoral, nor idolaters, nor adulterers, nor men who practice homosexuality, nor thieves, nor the greedy, nor drunkards, nor revilers, nor swindlers will inherit the kingdom of God."

His voice droned on, becoming louder. He interspersed "faggot" and "sinner" among the biblical words, as he leaned in closer and shouted into the young man's ear.

Ezekiel lifted a whip, and a lump mixed with sour saliva almost choked her. Several leather thongs sprouted from the handle, each one's end embedded with a metal weight. The flail swished through the air, the sound sickening her. Bits of torn skin flew up with each stroke. She ran across the cell and grasped the bars. "Stop, you bastards!"

Ezekiel focused on the task in hand, oblivious to her shouts or the boy's cries. The white of his wide eyes stood out of his red, mottled face like marbles. Demented and uncontrolled, he lifted the whip, beaming as the sharp metal weights sank into flesh again and again. More fragments of skin and sinew were ripped out as the man's arm went up and down, like a steam piston.

"Do not lie with a man as one lies with a woman. It's detestable!"

He struck the boy harder, with renewed energy. "You are a disgrace. Beg God for forgiveness!"

The young man didn't answer. She saw he was disorientated as he lapsed in and out of consciousness. His slight body shuddered and stilled. Was he dead?

Ezekiel's fury gained momentum, his voice shaking with insanity. Eamon Tierney caught his arm. "Stop, you'll kill him!"

Ezekiel shrugged him off, but finally stopped. "He deserves to die!"

A rivulet of sweat glistened as it trickled through the deep scar cut into his left cheek. He threw the flail to the floor and dragged a clean, white handkerchief across his forehead.

The group stood around the stone, staring down at Jonathan. Fremont Braxton prodded him with his toe. No response. He kicked him, then watched with indifference as the boy remained sprawled out, as still as a dead animal left by the wayside. The butcher yawned and stuck his hands in his pockets.

Xantara tore her gaze away from the boy and stared at her husband. There was sheer horror on his face. His jaw hung open, reminding her of a rendition of "The Scream." Time stood still as she searched his face, until the boy shrieked. She broke free from her trance and turned back to Jonathan. What now?

Ezekiel nodded a silent order. Eamon and Archie unclipped Jonathan's restraints and flipped him over like a rag doll. Fremont moved between the boy's legs and yanked his trousers down to his ankles, exposing a bush of fuzzy red hair framing a flaccid penis and shrunken testicles.

The butcher held his boning knife and sharpening block above the lad and drew them against each other, steel to steel. He dropped the block, tethered to his belt, and in one swift movement grabbed the boy's genitals and swept the knife down in a flashing arc. A chill consumed Xantara as he held his trophy high. She couldn't help but look down at the damage, and noticed how little blood dripped from the wound. Just a grotesque black slash gaping between his legs. The butcher wiped his knife on his apron, leaving a long, bloody line. He bent low over the boy. "I'll stop your vile practices, my boy."

She looked again at her husband as he raised a shaky hand to his forehead. He pulled at his collar, and flinched. His back straightened as his training kicked in and he strode forward to help the boy, but Ezekiel held him back.

Ezekiel nodded again at the two men. They released the chains, hauled his comatose body from the altar, and dumped him onto the cot like a piece of garbage. They pushed Braeden aside as he tried again to help the boy. The cell door clanged shut in his face, and they turned the lock.

Xantara's chin trembled as she shook her head in disbelief. They all terrified her. She could see they felt no regret; in fact they seemed to enjoy what they'd just done. Just what evil plans were they dreaming up for her? Her whole body quaked, her stomach churned, and she lurched forward, throwing up all over the stone flags. Acid bile rose into her throat as the smell of vomit and coppery blood made her gag again.

Scared stiff, she shrank back against the wall as they turned toward her.

CHAPTER TWO

Two weeks earlier

Imogene smiled up at her father and squeezed his hand as she danced down High Street. It wasn't often Daddy spent time with her. She skipped along, her spirits buoyed by the glorious sunshine and clear blue sky, thinking about the day ahead. She remembered the first time she and Mommy had seen the lake. The island in its center was mysterious. Maybe there were dragons that breathed fire, and maidens in distress. Today she would find out.

"I think the island is magical, Daddy."

"I'm sure it is, Sweetie. Have a good time."

She threw her arms around him and puckered her lips. Braeden kissed her and gave her a bear hug, then tickled her chin. "Have a wonderful day, sugar plum. I'll pick you up this afternoon."

She waved at school friends who waited at the wharf. Miss Stevenson, her teacher, had promised the nature lesson as an end-of-term treat, and she couldn't wait to explore.

Miss Stevenson smiled, looked down her list, and ticked off Imogene's name. She tucked the clipboard under her arm and grabbed Imogene's hand to steady her as they navigated the narrow gangway onto the ferry.

Imogene tossed her dark blonde ponytail to behind her shoulder as she hopped off the gangplank and made her way down the aisle. Her best friend Sophie patted the seat beside her. "Sit here, isn't this great?" Imogene's eyes sparkled as she chatted with her classmates.

Water slapped against the boat flanks making it rock, and the motion enchanted her. The skipper turned a key, the engine caught, and they were off.

She turned this way and that, drinking in the sights. Birds ducked and dived as they followed the boat. Together, she and Sophie looked over the side. Perhaps they would see fish. But the boat wake disturbed the water, obscuring the view. They gave up and watched the birds instead.

The children cheered as the boat moored alongside the rickety dock. Miss Stevenson lined them up and led them along the well-trodden path toward the ruins. As they drew closer Imogene saw two stone rooms that looked still intact, overshadowed by a huge tower which reminded her of Rapunzel's story, one of her favorites.

She looked at the ruins, then frowned back at the village. Miss Stevenson had said that the structure had been built over the remains of an Anglo-Saxon settlement, which the Normans later improved. She hinted the entire region might be riddled with tunnels, perhaps some that linked the island to the village.

Before long the group sat on a bank outside the ruins, notebooks and crayons in hand.

"Let's sketch the birds and butterflies," Miss Stevenson said. "Look— see that red admiral darting around? And there—there's one drinking sap from a gorse bush."

Imogene sat transfixed, as she watched the butterflies flitting among the bright yellow patches of gorse that decorated the island like ornaments on a Christmas tree. She selected a deep red crayon that matched the wings, drew a butterfly shape on her notebook, and colored within the wings. She held out her sketch and studied it. She liked her work to be perfect. She reshaped the wings, then completed her picture with a yellow crayon.

Miss Stevenson called the class together at lunchtime and doled out dry fish paste sandwiches with curled edges, followed by plastic mugs filled with watery orange juice. She topped the meal off with bananas.

"Class, we'll have a short break, then explore the island. No one is to wonder off, is that clear?"

"Yes, Miss Stevenson."

The teacher moved a few yards away, opened her cell phone, and punched the keys. She tucked a stray tendril of mousy brown hair behind her ear and leaned against a tree, her back turned to the children.

"Bet she's phoning her boyfriend," Sophie whispered.

The lads started an impromptu game of cricket; using sticks for the wicket and a book for the bat. They shrieked and laughed as they made their runs. The girls sat in a circle making daisy chains, draping them around their necks and on their heads. They fashioned smaller chains into bracelets and anklets, and giggled as they modeled their creations down an imaginary catwalk.

Imogene made her daisy chains, then sat nearby, watching the parade. Full from her meal, she lay back and relaxed, and dreamt of fairies and butterflies. The sun's rays warmed her cheeks and she smiled as pictures filled her mind.

She sensed a slight movement and opened one eye. A red admiral fluttered above her. She sat up and watched it fly over the wall. Fascinated, she set off after it, and before long she was deep inside the fortress. She lost sight of her quarry.

As she searched for the creature she heard a low moan and froze, her head cocked to listen. She heard it again, and went to investigate. She slipped through an open archway and walked toward the small rooms she'd spotted earlier. The moans, originating deep inside the chamber, grew louder. She followed the sounds into the dark shadows cast by the tower.

"Who's there?"

She couldn't see where the sound came from, and bit her lip as she looked around. A loud crack cut through the air above her. Her head jerked back as she looked toward a gap in the roof, and saw heavy stones rain down. She tried to cry out, but the sound caught in her throat, silenced forever. Her world darkened, and she knew no more.

Shelley Stevenson felt the shock waves as the rocks hit the ground, then heard the children yell out. She snapped her phone shut and rounded them up. "Kids, we'd better get back to the boat. The building sounds unstable."

They wailed in protest. "But we want to explore," Sophie said.

"I'm sorry. We'll come another time. Please get in line."

She counted the children as they boarded the boat. "We're missing someone," she said. She called the roll. "Imogene's gone." She turned to the skipper. "Please watch the children, I must go find her."

The skipper saluted, and she made her way back onto the island. She saw no sign of Imogene. The grass slope was empty, and she wasn't in the grove of trees. She scoured the ruins, being careful not to touch any walls. She moved into the smaller room, and jerked her head back and gasped. A pile of rocks had fallen toward the back, and a small white hand stuck up from it, like a flag of surrender.

Her hand flew to her throat. "Oh, my God!" She squeezed her eyes shut, and her muscles stiffened. "It can't be." At last she forced herself to move, and ran toward the child.

She scrambled up the rocks and heaved and pushed at them, but they were too heavy. She ignored her bleeding shins and broken nails as she tried again, and again. It was impossible! She stopped and looked around for a lever, but there was none. Her best efforts had made little if any impression. It was useless.

Clouds of pungent dust made it difficult to breathe. She pressed her blouse to her mouth and gasped as she slumped across the pile. With great effort she reached out and touched the child's hand, and screamed. Was that someone else yelling? Someone in pain, faraway, a soul in torment? The noise resonated in her head until she realized it came from her own mouth.

How could a single moment of inattention end in such tragedy? How stupid, irresponsible and senseless! She swallowed, her chin quivered, and guilt overwhelmed her.

She fell silent. After a while she became aware of the skipper's hand on her shoulder, encouraging her to release the child. She stared straight ahead as she clutched the child's hand in a death grip, and he pried her fingers off, one by one. She fell against him as he led her away, and looked back. The hand seemed bizarre, disembodied. It looked as if it belonged in a horror movie.

The skipper draped her arm around his shoulder and guided her away. She barely noticed as he settled her down in the ferry and covered her with his cable knit jersey. He entered the wheelhouse and picked up the marine radio mike. She frowned. He must be calling the police and ambulance services.

She turned back toward the children. They huddled together, half the benches empty. Sobs racked little Sophie's chest as she looked back toward the ruin.

"Where's Imogene?"

No one answered.

Before long a police launch swept into the inlet, and docked beside the ferry. Two officers boarded and talked to the skipper.

They tried to question her, but she couldn't speak. She sobbed, muttering, "my God, my God," over and over. Her mind was stuck in a loop that she couldn't break.

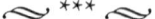

Sergeant Thomas and his constable ran along the path toward the tower. When they saw the stiff, white hand, they looked at each other. It was too late. They made a half-hearted attempt to move some of the stones, but soon stopped. It might be prudent leave the site undisturbed.

Both men were fathers, and the horrific sight made them queasy, the skin around their eyes bunched as they stared. The Sergeant nodded and blinked. "Nothing we can do here," he said. "Better get the kids home."

He left the young constable behind on guard duty. It was a potential crime scene, after all. He jumped into the police launch and signaled the ferry's skipper, who fired his engine and followed him back to shore. As the sergeant guided his launch toward the village, he radioed the station to organize the recovery.

As he approached the dock, he saw that parents were already gathering at the dock. The whole village must have heard his launch's shrill siren as it careened toward the island. He pulled up beside the wharf, leaving room for the ferryboat.

Two fathers climbed aboard and helped the children off. One by one they fell into their mothers' arms, faces white with shock. The families soon left with their children, eager no doubt to reach the safety of home. A lone man still waited, his eyes searching the vessel from aft to stern.

The sergeant jumped off the launch, secured the line, and went ashore, his face grave as he walked toward Doctor Braeden Pembroke. The father's knees buckled as he apparently realized the truth. It was his child. The sergeant grasped the doctor's shoulder to steady him, and broke the terrible news.

Shelley Stevenson watched the sergeant approach the doctor, and panicked. She looked around. What should she do? A policewoman climbed aboard and took her hand, and led her ashore.

"Where do you live?"

She pointed up the street, and they walked that direction. Her familiar pale yellow front door came into view. All she wanted was to go in, climb into bed, and pull the covers over her head. Perhaps it would all turn out to be a nightmare.

They entered and she sat at the dining room table and rubbed the back of her neck. She heard the officer go into the kitchen and put the kettle on, returning with a pot of English breakfast tea. She sat opposite her and poured the hot liquid into two cups.

"Milk? Sugar?"

"Just milk, please."

The teaspoon rattled against the cup as Miss Stephenson's hand shook. How on earth could she tell the parents? She blamed herself. She'd cautioned the class to stay put, but she shouldn't have taken her eyes off them. Not for one second, not for a moment.

The tea ritual calmed her down, and she looked up. The policewoman appeared kind, and she relaxed.

"Tell me what happened, exactly. Every step, from when you boarded the boat."

It was hard to describe, and before long she developed a headache. It pounded harder as she worried about the consequences. Would they blame her? What a way to die! How could she have been so stupid, so foolish? It took just a few minutes.

The policewoman stood. "I'll leave you to get some rest. Perhaps tomorrow we can talk again."

She answered her in a monotone. "The school board chose Imogene for the gifted child program, you know. Such an intelligent girl and a hard worker, and now that potential is lost through my negligence. How will I live with it?"

Imogene floated above the ruins. She watched Miss Stevenson strain and wrench rocks from the pile. Why was she here? As she wondered, she found herself just above the teacher. She was flying, she realized with delight, as she swooped up and back down. Wow, this was great. Her attention went back to her teacher. Where were the others?

As she moved closer she saw her teacher grab a hand, a small hand, surrounded by rocks. "Miss Stevenson what're you doing?"

She didn't hear her. She tried again.

"Whose hand is that?"

Still, no response. She moved closer.

The wrist had a daisy chain around it, and a silver bracelet, its links made up of alternate stars and crescent moons. It was her bracelet, she recognized it straight away. What did that mean? She held up her wrist. It was bare. She flew up, then down, and hovered. Yes, it was her bracelet.

The skipper arrived and led her teacher away. She floated higher, toward the boat. The kids look upset. What's happened? Her friend Sophie looked distraught. Imogene floated down and put her arm around her, watched it passed right through. She tried again without success. She must be a ghost. Perhaps she was dead, but it didn't worry her. She felt fine.

She watched the police launch arrive, and followed the two policemen to the tower. They looked at the arm sticking through the rocks, and tried to move some. They looked sad, and she wondered why. What happened? The taller man went back toward his boat, and the younger policeman settled on a smooth rock a few feet away from the arm.

Imogene remembered the hand, and drifted back over the rock pile. Yes, that was her bracelet, and it looked like her hand. In alarm, she looked down at her body. It appeared wispy, not solid. Fear crept into her soul, like an icy finger. Something's wrong. She brought her hands up to her head. She felt the same as ever, but she didn't look normal.

A movement caught her eye, and a woman appeared beside her. Who was she? A little scared, she flew a few yards away. The lady followed, smiling. She was beautiful. Reassured, Imogene calmed down. The woman shimmered as her iridescent clothes floated around her. Pale hair framed her delicate features, reminding her of her mother.

"Are you an angel?"

"Perhaps," the lady said. "Come, I have wonderful places to show you."

She held out her hand, and Imogene took it. They flew side by side through a bright passageway that opened before them.

"Are we going to Heaven?"

CHAPTER THREE

Ezekiel's boat cut a swathe through the water as he raced away from the island, his engine roaring as he pushed it to the limit. He tipped his head back and peered at the sky.

"Thank you, Jesus!"

He punched his fist in the air, and his eyes blazed with fervor. "At last! You gave me the opportunity, and I carried out your will!"

He watched his wife hurry down the garden path as he clambered out of his boat onto his private jetty. She was a tiny woman, almost bird-like, with wispy, dry silvery hair outlining her face. Her lips pursed in annoyance. He knew she wasn't irritated at that moment, but over the years he'd watched the expression etch permanently onto her face. As she clumped along the path in her sensible brown brogues she played with a string of pearls hanging around her neck that complemented her soft cream blouse and calf-long tweed skirt. She stopped and jutted out her turkey chin.

"Well?"

Ezekiel beamed. "Just as the Good Lord foretold, it went well."

"What happened?"

"Let's go inside, it's good news."

As they walked along the gravel path that meandered through his manicured lawn, Ezekiel admired their house ahead. The former rectory's perfect proportions were covered in ivy, and would grace any calendar without shame. The driveway swept in a circle past the front entrance, and tall Georgian windows set in pale grey stone looked regal across the facade. He'd read the bricks had been excavated from a Cotswold quarry a century earlier, and carried down by wagon.

Millicent made a pot of Earl Grey tea and placed it on an antique card table her father had brought it back from India, after he'd finished his commission as an officer in the Lancers. She'd always loved the inlaid ivory top and the handsome carved elephants that graduated down the legs, so he'd allowed her to keep it despite its pagan associations.

"The Lord enticed her into the ruin with a butterfly," he said. "I obeyed Him, and she is dead. One more of Satan's offspring has been removed from God's earth."

His wife lifted the delicate China cup to her lips. "Praise the Lord! How pleased He must be."

"Yes, Amen!"

She reached across the table and squeezed his hand. "I'm so proud of you."

"Thank you, but I'll be happier when we've dealt with her mother. Such wickedness should not be allowed. Such a vile creature shouldn't breathe the same air as God's elect. It's intolerable, an abomination!"

Later, his wife settled into her comfortable chintz chair and reached down to her mending basket. She pulled a rough flour sack from its depths, then threaded her needle. With care, she stitched small fishhooks an inch apart in rows down the sack as she hummed her favorite hymn. "I come to thee, dear Lord."

Ezekiel gave her a perfunctory peck. "I have to sign documents at the office, dear," he said. He touched the row of hooks, a slow smile spreading across his face.

He was proud of his positions as the village lawyer and Justice of the Peace. He knew everyone's business. Working with seven villages kept him busy. A client was due to have a will finalized, and perhaps he could glean a little of the estate. He picked up his car keys.

As he drove his silver Jaguar into Monkton St Michael and saw the villagers stare at him, he realized again that they were wary of him. They said he strutted, and called him the Cockerel, but he didn't mind. It meant they respected him. His tall stature gave him an added advantage, and the people were overawed. He knew long ago they would bend like willow branches to please him, and he manipulated them with ease.

He parked in front of the post office in the dead center of High Street and made his way up the stairs to his private sanctorum above it, walked to the window, and rested against the sill. What a perfect view! He looked down on his subjects as they milled about below. Their secrets hovered above their heads in word balloons, and he knew every one of them. He stroked his shiny bald dome and gave himself a subconscious pat on the back. "How great I am! God has chosen me!" It was his daily mantra.

He was superior, with legitimate reason. He walked with God, was one of the elect. His group's deluded members assumed they would join him in a glorious afterlife, but they could never be good enough. He laughed aloud. The Lord favored him and his wife, and had given them profitable businesses and a beautiful home. They were blessed, indeed.

Would his minions instigate the Lord's work, as he did? No! They were followers, robots without sense. But he loved God's assignments. In fact, he relished them.

He sat at his desk and spread his hands over the beautiful green leather inlay which was tooled with an elegant gold border, then touched the heavy antique brass ink set that rested on top. He twirled his Mont Blanc pen between finger and thumb, reluctant to start work.

He pressed a button under the desk and a secret door slid open. He pulled out a small black notebook filled with distinctive, cramped script, made new entries, and read the contents. It was a list of people's names and their sins. He awarded each violation a numerical value, seven points for adultery, and a mere three points for theft. He totaled the sinners' grades each day.

Xantara Pembroke's name was at the top.

Today, he had made significant strides. With the Lord's help she'd received the punishment she deserved. He rocked his chair back, then leaned forward and put a line through the first name under hers. Imogene Pembroke.

Yes, this day marked a turning point in his service to the Lord. He knew his Master lured her there. He had waited for weeks for this breakthrough, was ecstatic when she finally followed the butterfly into the chamber. Burn, little girl, burn! Yes, the fires of Hell would burn bright and hot today.

He leaned back once more and put his hands behind his head, and his eyes glazed over as he re-experienced that glorious sense of euphoria as the rocks rained down, silencing the devil's spawn forever.

Soon it would be her mother's turn. Mrs. Pembroke couldn't imagine the punishments poised to rain down on her. The destruction of Sodom and Gomorrah was child's play, compared with his methods of chastisement. His face flushed as he reveled in the many ways he would punish her.

Two nights later, Ezekiel's elite group gathered in his drawing room. As he watched them arrive he reflected over the years taken to build this collection of souls. It was hard work, shaping them to his will, but worth it now that they were all devoted to God's Truth. Now, when he simply raised his little finger, they salivated as they awaited his next order.

His chin jutted out, his legs planted wide apart. "Welcome folks, come in. Let us celebrate the Lord tonight."

The hand-picked followers were, in his mind, weak-minded parishioners, easy prey. Pastor Mark Benedict, of course, wasn't there. He didn't realize the little group's true nature, and his inherent faith in people's goodness blinded him from the truth. Ezekiel frowned as he thought of this. He'd soon have to deal with Mark and his wife Florence. He found it tiresome to pussyfoot around the man day after day, but he would be patient. He would plan carefully and choose the right time, then deal with them. And soon.

Millicent arranged the chairs into a circle and signaled for them to sit, and Ezekiel motioned for silence. He opened the meeting with prayer, and the two couples and the butcher obediently bowed their heads. After the prayer he paused for effect, and felt a warm glow inside as he looked around the group.

"The Lord was with me," he said. "The deed is done."

He laughed, then told how the child's death unfolded. He paused as his followers applauded, then progressed with other urgent business.

"As you know, the mother is practicing witchcraft," he said. "We've seen her with other women in Avebury Circle. They dress in robes, beat drums, then no doubt invoke the Devil. I won't tolerate this behavior in our villages. I'll deal with the entire coven, but first we must cut off the snake's head."

"Hear, hear."

He hated Xantara Pembroke, and knew they did, too, but he had to make sure they followed the plan. The daughter's murder was the first step to her downfall. Now they had to groom the husband.

"We must give him sympathy," he said. We must cook him meals, do other things." He handed a list to Ethel Redford. "Start first thing tomorrow."

After the group left, Ezekiel poured a glass of malt whisky. The amber liquid gleamed as the cut-glass facets reflected the firelight. He sat contemplating how to use the father's grief to indoctrinate him into their group. Not Xantara, of course, she wasn't redeemable. His plan for her was special, special indeed. He rubbed his hands together as he allowed himself a few pleasant daydreams.

Ezekiel's eyelids popped open. One problem, of course, was that the man was an atheist. He thought about that, and smiled. But then, of course, he, Ezekiel, was persuasive. He checked the front door, slid the deadbolt into place, then stood for a moment. A familiar voice whispered in his ear.

"Go to your prayer room for further instructions, my son."

He snapped to attention and hurried up the stairs. The Lord must want to congratulate him!

Chapter Four

Braeden stood, feet planted, arms crossed, in front of the ramp. "I'm going, even if I have to swim."

The sergeant backed up. "Sir, it's bad, you don't want to see her as she is. Wait until we recover the body." He glanced away. "Sorry, I meant to say, until we bring your daughter back to shore."

Braeden's heart raced, and his eye twitched. "Look, I've worked the emergency department, there's little I haven't seen. What if another rock fall injures someone? Another doctor could take hours to get here."

The officer's chin fell. "Okay, let's go." He stepped aside.

Braeden leaned against the wheelhouse, his mouth dry, as he stared toward the island. When the launch touched the dock he jumped out and strode along the path, his face grim, as the others followed. They stopped at the rock pile. He was shocked at the incongruous sight of his daughter's precious hand atop the heap.

He stared in disbelief at Imogene's tiny hand. It's true! She's gone. His stomach felt queasy and his mind blanked, as emotions churned through his body. He couldn't look away. He swayed and reached for the keep wall, and watched the police move the rocks. He wanted to help, but his body was paralyzed. "It can't be true! Not my baby girl," he whispered. He knees collapsed and he slipped down the wall.

The men moved the rocks carefully, to prevent further damage to the body. Many were so large it took three men to carry them. Several times debris fell and the men scattered, fearing a fresh rock fall. Dust clouds made the scene move in and out of focus. It took almost two hours for them to uncover his daughter's body.

Her crushed and lifeless body, broken and twisted, lay at unnatural angles. He started toward her, and a constable blocked him. Medics pushed past and knelt beside her, and one put his fingers to her neck. It was clear his daughter was beyond mortal help, but Braeden supposed they had protocols to follow. He shrank into himself, his body visibly smaller, his gaze fixed. He drew on his reserves and pulled himself together for the sake of his daughter.

"Are you all right, sir?" an officer asked.

Was the man crazy? What a stupid question! Of course he wasn't all right. "I'll be okay," he said.

He found it difficult to connect that broken body with the child he knew so well. Visions of a vibrant, talented girl rushed in, of her laughing as he bounced her on his knee. She held her arms out at the pool, confident he would catch her as she jumped. It was his duty to protect her. And he'd failed. She was always a daddy's girl. It was unbearable to imagine that love broken and gone forever. Acid burned his throat, and he fought the urge to vomit.

Old feelings of grief resurfaced. He thought of his parents, both dead when he was just thirteen. Anger and helplessness from that time merged with the fresh grief that overwhelmed him now. Images of their broken bodies rushed into his consciousness. Not now, I can't take it!

Memories of other families he'd seen as a doctor also flooded his mind. He saw them sitting with their dead children behind half-drawn curtains in the emergency room. Many times he had broken the news that their child wouldn't be going home. They usually didn't cry and wail as the movies depicted, they were too traumatized. Now he was the one in shock.

He'd dealt with many cases of children's accidental deaths, but this was his own daughter! It couldn't be real! His throat was full, as if his Adam's apple had migrated. He couldn't even pray. He'd lost his belief in God many years before.

He thought about his wife and her joy at Imogene's birth. How would she survive? Imogene, her youngest, the little girl she'd dreamt of for years. After the unexpected arrival of his son Alistair halfway through his internship, they'd waited a full fourteen years before their second child. They were on a high for months.

A flash from the police photographer's camera jolted him back. He watched the man take pictures from every angle, and every flash stabbed his heart. He was anxious to catch a last glimpse of her, to touch her, to hold her.

He pushed forward. "I need to see her."

The policeman stepped aside and he stumbled over to her body, knelt, and stroked her golden hair, matted with blood. "My baby," he whispered. "I love you so much." As he looked at her body, he noticed her crushed and twisted pelvis. His eyes focused on that promise of womanhood, a sacred space that would never feel the joy, the first flutter of new life inside it. All he wanted was to gather her to him, mend her broken body, beg for a miracle. Have his daughter back.

The officer in charge drew Braeden away. They started to cover her body with a khaki tarpaulin, but he stopped them. "Just a few minutes." They stepped back and allowed him access.

He drew the sheet back and brushed his lips against her forehead. Already she felt icy cold. Although the summer sun beat down on his back, his soul seemed as cold and still as hers. He allowed the cover to fall back and staggered away. A constable helped him back to the launch.

He stood against the wheelhouse door, almost unaware of the strong breeze that blew his hair straight back, as he thought about Xantara. How could he tell her? He wished the trip back would never end. The future seemed unbearable.

How could this have happened? Why was she in the ruins, alone? The rocks had stood intact for hundreds of years, why choose today to fall? He should have gone with them! He could never have imagined such a beautiful day would turn into such a nightmarish afternoon.

He stiffened as he remembered. Xantara would be back soon. Too soon.

CHAPTER FIVE

Xantara tapped the steering wheel in time to the music as she drove along the familiar country lanes toward Avebury. She enjoyed the wild summer flowers that filled the hedgerows, and hummed in time with the radio. Imogene's eagerness to see the island had lifted her own heart. Life couldn't be better.

The closer she got to her birthplace, the more she felt its mystical power. She always imagined a silver cord binding her to its energy field.

Her thoughts drifted back to how her eighteenth birthday had changed her life. Her mother had taken her to her initiation ceremony at the ancient stone circle. She became an Energy Guardian, and received the powers that came with that office.

A few months later she moved to a flat in Swindon to attend the Polytechnic. She loved every moment of her nursing course, and three years later became a licensed midwife. It had been her childhood dream, and hard work turned it into reality, making her mom proud.

Part of her degree required her to work in a hospital, and it was there she met Braeden. She smiled as she remembered their first date at the local Irish pub. Boy, was he handsome! They became inseparable and married as soon as she started work.

He was surprised to learn she was an albino, as her eyes were a brilliant turquoise blue, ringed with a deep green. A normal albino's irises were translucent, almost colorless, except for a light pink caused by blood flowing through veins beneath the surface.

She'd smiled, unable to tell him why she was different. For centuries Avebury had produced albinos, but now she was the only one in this generation.

Her unusual powers helped her work at the baby clinic, making it easy to form strong connections with mothers and their babies. Her ability to calm a crying infant coupled with her sharp insight had saved more than one child. Intuition was an incredible gift, she was so blessed.

The long hours she worked to support them both seemed worth it. Braeden continued his internship and took several specialist courses, then chose to work in the emergency department. The pressure and pain day after day drained him, and he'd jumped at the chance to move to Monkton St Michael.

The mammoth stones of Avebury came into view and pulsed as she drove by. The monoliths surrounded the village, and the main road ran straight through the middle. She passed the chocolate-box cottages and headed out toward Sudbury Hill.

Her friend Bryony lived in a picturesque cottage near the hill. Xantara's face softened as she thought about their lifelong friendship. Although they weren't alike, their differences enriched their rapport. Then, of course, the ancient secrets they shared bonded them closer than sisters.

As she passed the outer circle, she noted her special place. It was where she spent time alone, to nourish her soul and connect with the spirit realm. She craved solitude, and came here to meditate and deepen her abilities. She received messages from the ancient ones at the portal stones, and guidance that helped her perform healing rites.

Bryony opened the door, they hugged, and went inside. "Everyone's here," she said. Xantara greeted the other seven women and took her seat at the scrubbed kitchen table. The small kitchen was a squeeze, but they didn't mind. They were family.

Xantara regarded her best friend as she sat opposite her, an attractive woman of medium build with deep auburn hair. She favored long print dresses, and today a cascade of brilliant beads adorned her multi-colored frock. Yes, she was a wild child, and if born a few years earlier she would have made a splendid hippie. Xantara loved her open and easy ways, and her quirkiness. A friendship linked by the cosmos, as well as shared ancestry.

The eight Energy Guardians joined hands in accordance with their sect's ancient doctrines, and recited their creed in unison.

"Creator of the Cosmos we acknowledge you, and ask for your presence here today. Giver-of-life and health, we thank you for your goodness. We accept your Universal authority. We submit to your will, through your power, and promise to love, heal and protect humanity from all wickedness."

Xantara listened to the words that had been recited for almost five thousand years, beginning with the original guardians who erected the Avebury circle. Their purpose was to protect and use the powerful stones, which had a unique energy that released undreamt-of power when sacred ceremonies were performed.

The fire blazed in the hearth, despite being summer. The cottage's thick stone walls took time to warm up after the cool night. She liked a cheerful fire, one that jumped and crackled. They each nursed a mug of hot chocolate and helped themselves from a plate of lemon tarts. The guardians were in a good mood, the conversation thought-provoking and energetic.

"I've heard Mrs. Cowley has gout." Callista looked around. "It's painful, and she could do with our help."

A discussion followed, and the women decided to heal her during the next full moon. The energy needed time to build, and reached its peak on the night of the full moon. It was even stronger at the equinox. That's when they tackled difficult cases.

Xantara assigned their tasks, so they could prepare for preliminary rituals before the main event. Dorcas, the herbalist, had the most work to do, preparing the potions.

Xantara reflected on her position as the doctor's wife. She was the first to hear of villagers' ailments, and advised the group of serious cases. This year she was also the leader and primary energy producer. She enjoyed the position, but the role sapped her reserves, so a year was the maximum she was allowed to serve.

They discussed the more intricate preparations needed to activate the stone's potent energy. Mrs. Cowley's case was simple, since she was a local, understood their work, and needed no explanations.

Xantara sat at the table enjoying time with her friends, until she began to feel uneasy. First she noticed her shoulders tense, then her stomach flutter. The disquiet turned to fear and then dread. Something was wrong. She glanced over her shoulder toward the door. It was time she headed home.

She stood. "Sorry, but I must go, see you next week." She gave each of her friends a quick hug.

Bryony walked her to the door. "You look worried." She embraced her again. "What's wrong?"

"I just feel weird, something isn't right."

Bryony nodded and puckered her brow. "Please ring me as soon as you get home."

"I will, I promise."

She sped along the narrow lanes toward home, her imagination running wild. What's wrong? Her speed increased and she raced dangerously around blind corners.

The silent main street spooked her. Where was everyone? She parked and hurried to the house. The clinic door was locked, the closed sign showing. Her palms sweated as she unlocked it. Where were Braeden, the patients? Perplexed, she went back into their living quarters, stood stock-still, and listened. A strange, strangled wail came from the upstairs bedroom. What was that? Her stomach twisted and contracted in pain.

Reluctantly, she climbed the stairs. She didn't want to reach the bedroom, not yet. What's happened? Her steps slowed as a wave of fear caught her unaware. Her instinct told her that her world was about to fall apart.

Braeden looked up as she entered the room, his eyes red. Utter devastation showed on his face like a barren moonscape, dry, empty.

"Imogene?" she whispered.

He nodded, and they fell into each other's arms.

Xantara was frantic to see her daughter. The ambulance had taken her to Swindon Hospital, and she was in the basement morgue. She drove. Braeden seemed incapable of rational behavior, and a crash was the last thing they needed. Now and then she glanced at him as they travelled in silence, their throats too constricted to speak. He kept shaking his head, his hands clenching in his lap.

Forty minutes later they arrived at the hospital entrance and went in. The charge nurse paged the morgue attendant, who came up by lift to escort them. Xantara shuddered as she looked at the enormous refrigerator that stored the unfortunate, lifeless bodies. The attendant slid a stainless steel drawer out, one of many banked across the wall.

Imogene was covered with a sheet, her tiny toes poked out at the bottom. The man peeled off the green cotton cover and stood aside. Shocked into silence, Xantara dropped a kiss on her daughter's cold lips. Imogene's eyelashes were shiny. Xantara knew they used Vaseline to keep eyelids shut. Her daughter's face was as white as fresh snow, her cute rosebud lips now colorless.

She imagined her beautiful sky-blue eyes hidden behind the closed lids. She would never see them sparkle again. A sigh escaped her lips, her heart heavy as she touched her cheek. She looked frozen, so lifeless, like a doll. All she wanted to do is to pick her up and run from the hospital, to find some way to keep her.

She didn't want to leave, but heard the attendant's foot tap behind her. Her body sagged, and she turned and walked away. As she stepped through the mortuary door she fell into Braeden's arms.

Since the cause of death was clear, the coroner decided against an autopsy. He signed a release and the undertakers moved the child to their chapel of rest. Xantara went to see her again. They'd placed her small coffin in a viewing room on a trolley, a white plastic chair beside it. She sank into the seat, then inspected Imogene's face, trying to commit each detail to memory. Blue tinged her white face around the lips and eyes. The funeral director had combed her hair and dressed her in clothes they had requested from Xantara earlier. The mortician had burned the dirty, torn clothing from the accident.

Imogene wore a cornflower blue dress trimmed with white lace. Embroidered white socks decorated with tiny pink bows covered her feet. Her grandmother's star-shaped locket hung around her neck. The undertaker had arranged her hands as if in prayer. The white rose he'd placed between her fingers filled the air with a delicate scent.

Her daughter looked different. It was obvious her soul had left, her lifeblood long stilled. Imogene's spirit was gone. The body was just an empty shell.

"I love you so much, precious. I know we'll be together again." Tears wouldn't come, the shock had stilled her grief. She believed in an afterlife, but that didn't help ease the pain caused by the loss of her daughter's physical presence in this world.

 ***

They held the funeral a week later at the church on the hill, St Michaels. The diocese granted special permission to bury her in the churchyard, the first internment there for seventy years. Xantara was grateful. She didn't believe in cremation, and the thought of her daughter consumed by an electric furnace was abhorrent.

The whole village turned out for the service, and provided a buffet for the wake in the school hall. Xantara stayed for twenty minutes, then slipped out unnoticed. She wanted solitude and peace, to be alone, to grieve in private. She couldn't tolerate the people's sympathetic faces, since they made her loss a reality.

Over the next few days, she and Braeden acted like automatons. The village people were kind and sympathetic, but she knew they were glad it wasn't their child. They both noticed how many villagers crossed the street to avoid them when they stepped outside. Involvement with death through their work helped them realize the people didn't know what to say or how to respond. But it still hurt.

Church groups delivered meals to their door, more than they could eat even if they had an appetite. Most of them ended in her freezer. How did they think she could eat, when Imogene would never enjoy a meal again?

Xantara loved to sit by the lake, to watch the sunset over the water, but guilt denied her even this simple pleasure. Her daughter wasn't able to enjoy her life, so how could she? She decided she would never savor life again, in fact she at times even considered suicide. She wanted the pain to stop, but knew it never would.

The villagers had no idea how her daughter's death would affect their children's future, but she knew. This unprecedented event had never happened before, not in five thousand years, and now the chain was broken for good.

What were the guardians going to do?

CHAPTER SIX

Braeden bent over his desk and laid his head on his arms. He was tired, and hadn't slept well for nights. Tonight he would take a sleeping tablet to help cope with work.

He lifted his head and stared at the photo of Imogene at the beach, holding a bucket and spade. He pressed it to his lips and tears formed, spotting the silver frame. He pulled out his handkerchief, wiped his eyes, and set the photo down.

There was one more patient to see. Ezekiel had insisted on an after-hours appointment, claiming the waiting room was a germ bath. Braeden didn't approve, but knew he would lose patients if he didn't agree. He was certain Ezekiel would order the villagers to boycott his clinic, forcing them to drive all the way to the Avebury clinic. Why the villagers treated the man like a demi-god, he had no idea.

Five minutes after the last patient left, the outer door rattled. Braeden was sure Ezekiel had watched from his office across the street. The man blustered in and positioned his ample buttocks in the chair.

"What can I do for you?" Braeden asked.

"Usual. I want blood pressure and cholesterol medication."

Braeden was struck afresh by the deep baritone voice that filled the room, and could see how it would command respect. No wonder the locals obeyed him. He was a born orator.

Braeden brought up the prescriptions on his computer, printed and signed them, and handed them to Ezekiel. But the man didn't move from his chair. Instead he relaxed back into it, as if planning to stay a long time.

"How are you, Braeden?"

"As well as can be expected." Braeden eyed the door, as if planning an escape.

"Do you believe in God?"

Braeden slumped back in his chair. "Why do you ask? I'm a scientist, first and foremost. I'd like to think Imogene still exists somewhere, but I don't."

Ezekiel stared, his eyes hypnotic. "You're wrong. Let me explain the truth to you."

Braeden shifted in his chair and shut down his computer for the night. "If you must, but I don't think it will change my mind."

Over the next two hours, Ezekiel explained the tenants of Christianity, belief in God, Heaven, and Hell. Braeden yawned. All he wanted was sleep, but his curiosity kept him alert, anxious to learn more. He knew most of it from his childhood. His Catholic family went to church and he attended a Catholic school, but he gave up religion a long time ago. Unbidden memories from that time crept in. He remembered how clean and forgiven he felt after confession. He must admit he missed that.

As Ezekiel cajoled and persuaded, he felt himself weaken. The charismatic lawyer mixed science and religion in a compelling way. But was it the truth?

"Let me tell you about Heaven. It's a city paved with gold, adorned with jewels of every kind. There is no sorrow, no pain. Everyone is joyful, one big, happy family."

"Do you believe my daughter is there, and happy?"

Ezekiel avoided the question. "Let's meet after hours for the next few nights, to talk further," he said.

Braeden's lip quivered, his soul cried out for hope. Even a glimmer would help. He needed to believe his daughter's spirit lived on in another dimension. The idea of her body buried, rotting in a grave, was unbearable.

"Let's do it," he said.

Ezekiel left and Braeden sat alone, mulling over their conversation. His mind drifted back to his childhood and how grief had destroyed his faith.

****

Thirteen-year-old Braeden and his best friend William Guiney followed the priest as he swung the incense burner from side to side, its sweet, grey smoke blessing the congregation as it wafted over them. The altar boys, who attended the Catholic school and shared catechism classes, were dressed in deep crimson cassocks layered with lace-edged white cotton gowns. Their hands pressed together and heads bowed, they stood either side of Father Buchannan when he paused.

Braeden sensed the presence of God as the priest conducted mass. It was no longer in Latin, but the precious words suffused his soul. After mass he preceded Father Buchannan down the central aisle, and caught his mother's smile as he passed by.

She stood by Dad, soft and sweet in her pale lilac dress and angora cardigan. Dad wore a smart charcoal suit, set off by a cheerful yellow and navy tie, a Father's Day present. Afterwards, the crowd milled around in small groups, chatting. Others crowded around the priest deep in conversation, no doubt discussing confidential matters.

His parents arranged to meet another family for lunch at a nearby restaurant. They climbed into their light blue Hillman and Dad pulled out of the car park and turned right, toward the lights at the main junction. His father accelerated hard to beat the lights, looking straight ahead. As they crossed the intersection, there was a huge bang, and Braeden was thrown against the back of his mother's seat. He looked up. The front of the car was gone, and a splatter of blood covered the cracked windscreen. A horn blasted, people shouted, but inside the car it was silent.

Braeden's eyes widened. What had happened? His mother moaned, and he reached forward to grasp her shoulder. He realized another car had plowed into them from the side street.

"Don't worry Mom, you'll be alright."

She didn't answer but gasped for breath.

He looked across to his Dad, and stiffened. He yelped and covered his mouth. A metal rod protruding through the windscreen pierced his father's chest, and he was motionless, head slumped down, eyes open.

"Dad! Dad!" He shook his father's arm, but got no response.

Someone opened his door, and hands reached in. "Come along son, let me help you." It was Williams's father. He must have sprinted down the road as soon as he heard the noise. A siren cut through the air from the distance, and more people gathered. The commotion caused him to catch his breath as his stomach tensed. Someone helped him out of the car and he sat on the pavement, his jaw clenched.

"Help Mom! Leave me."

An ambulance pulled up, and two paramedics jumped out. They checked his Dad, then hurried round to check his Mother. Was his father dead?

His mom moaned. Within seconds, they were checking her vitals. Blood gushed from an artery at the top of her leg, and the medics stopped the flow with a compression pad. His forehead throbbed as he watched them stabilize her.

They put drips put in both arms and an oxygen mask on her bloodied face, then pulled a gurney from the ambulance. Sunlight glinted from polished steel as its scissor legs clicked down underneath. The medics lifted her onto it, covered her with a blanket, placed an oxygen bottle between her legs, and loaded the gurney to the ambulance.

One man stayed with her in the back, and the other jumped into the cab and switched the siren on. Chills ran down Braeden's spine as the siren screamed in the quiet Sunday street. As the ambulance shot off to the hospital, a second unit arrived. The paramedics hurried over to him and checked for injuries. Although his shins were bruised where they'd hit the seat back, he was unhurt.

"Is Mom all right?"

He knew his voice sounded small, so he repeated his question louder.

"Look, son, we need to take you to the hospital. They'll want to x-ray you, then you can see her, I'm sure." As he leaned on the medic for support to the ambulance, he saw William's dad whisper to the driver. Braeden climbed into the ambulance, and the man climbed in beside him

The medic draped a dark blue blanket around Braeden's shoulders, but it did little to relieve his shivers. Mr. Guiney drew him close, stroking his hair. He turned his face into the man's chest, trying to block out the vision of his dead father.

Mr. Guiney held him tighter. "It'll be okay, I'll take care of you. Of everything."

Braeden looked up and gripped the man's sweater. "No, you won't, you can't. Dad's dead!"

He noticed a thin red stripe woven into the rough woolen blanket as he fingered it. How inconsequential, he thought. "Inconsequential" was a new word he'd learnt in a recent English class. Now he really knew what it meant.

When they arrived at the hospital his mother was already in surgery, and they wouldn't let him see her. After x-rays they signed a release form and told him he could go.

"I want to see my mom," he said, staring at the closed door.

The nurse hugged him. "You poor child. She'll be in intensive care for some time."

Mr. Guiney put his arm around his shoulders. "I'll bring you back as soon as the doctor allows me to."

Mr. Guiney and his wife took him to their house and put him to bed. The family was kind, and their home was a comfortable, familiar place. The pain medications kicked in and he was soon fast asleep.

The next few days passed in a blur. Then before dawn one morning Mrs. Guiney woke him and they took him to the hospital. As the car moved through the empty streets, the quiet air felt strange to him. Sprays of rain glistened as they passed each streetlight. A doctor met them at the intensive care department and ushered him to a small room off the main ward.

A single table lamp lit up his mother's ashen face, merging it with the pillow's whiteness. He sat beside her and held her limp hand.

Her breathing was labored. "Son, I love you." She gasped for air. "I'll always watch over you… I promise, and I pray God will…take care of you." her eyes welled with tears. "I love you, son. I love you so much."

Her lids fluttered, then closed. A soft sigh escaped her parched lips and the pulse in her neck stopped.

Braeden flung himself over her body. "Mom! Don't go, Mom, I need you!"

The doctor left the room, apparently to give him time alone. He couldn't believe it! He'd lost his Dad, and now his Mom! This couldn't be happening. Was it a dream?

He left the room, to find the doctor with Father Buchannan and Mr. Guiney in the waiting room. He guessed the priest was there to give his mother last rites. The priest put an arm around his shoulder, but he shrugged it off.

"Braeden, let's pray for God's comfort, and absolution for your parents' souls."

Braeden pummeled the old man's chest. "I will never, ever, believe in God again!"

"Son, God loves you. He will always be there for you. Please pray with me."

"Never, never! They didn't deserve to die. If there is a God and he loves us, why did he take them? I will never believe in God again!"

~ *** ~

Night after night, he and Ezekiel sat in his office, talking. Hope grew in Braeden's heart. Why hadn't he heard this message before? For years he'd recited the catechism and attended mass, but never actually read the Bible. This man weaved science with religion together until the words felt right. Maybe they were true. Perhaps Imogene's soul survived.

Braeden's skepticism began to dissolve as he tossed the ideas around in his mind. As he listened over the next few nights, he found he could justify the existence of God alongside science and his medical knowledge. He wanted to seize the hope that his beloved daughter was alive and well in spirit, in a perfect place.

One night, after another long discussion, he turned to Ezekiel. "Thanks for the time you've spent to help me," he said. "It's a relief to know Imogene is in Heaven, and one day I'll see her again."

Ezekiel stood straight and cleared his throat. "As you know, your daughter wasn't a believer when she died. I hate to tell you, but she's in Hell right now."

Braeden's eyebrows raised. "What? How dare you say that, after you've finally given me hope?"

"Calm down, brother. We can change all that."

"How? What can we do?"

"If you accept Jesus into your heart as your Lord and Savior, we can pray for God to lift her up into Heaven."

"Let's do that!"

Ezekiel was silent for a moment. "There's a problem, though. Your wife."

"My wife?"

"You know about her activities in Avebury, don't you?"

"What activities? She visits her friends. They do have strange ideas, I'll give you that, but what of it?"

"Look, Braeden. They're involved in paganism and Satan worship. That must be stopped before we can plead mercy for your daughter."

He explained the shameful activities around the Avebury stone circle his sect members had witnessed. Braeden shook his head. Ezekiel pulled out his notebook and began to read from it.

"Head of a witch's coven…" He paused for effect. "Astrology, necromancy—she summons demons and contacts the dead. She is an evil woman."

Braeden couldn't believe it. Ezekiel showed him bible verses which detailed the abhorrent practices, and he read them with care. They were clear enough. How well did he know Xantara? She kept her little secrets, but…

"What can we do?" he asked

"My church group meets Thursday nights at St Michael's. Bring her along, and we'll talk with her. She'll renounce her evil ways when we point them out, I'm sure of it."

Ezekiel left and Braeden slumped in the chair, exhausted. What next?

At teatime after clinic on Thursday, Braeden put his cup down and stared at Xantara, strangely, she thought.

"Xantara, will you go to a church meeting with me?"

She eyed him. What was this sudden interest in religion? And why did Ezekiel spent so much time with her husband? She sensed his needs and wanted to help him. The day before he'd asked about Avebury and her friends, and she'd wondered why. She'd kept her role as Guardian from him because of his scientific mind-set, believing it best to downplay her spiritual side. Since the accident they'd sidestepped discussing their deepest feelings, as their views were so diverse. They tried not to hurt each other, or cause an argument.

"I thought you didn't believe in God," she said.

"I've thought about it, and I just can't accept Imogene's soul is gone."

"She isn't, love. Her spirit lives on, and one day we'll join her."

He nodded. "Well, I'm beginning to realize that's possible, but where is she?" He took a deep breath. "Let's go to the meeting this once, and see what they believe."

"Okay, if that's what you want."

She went upstairs to change. He'd soon get fed up with Ezekiel and his cronies, so what's the harm?

When they arrived at the church she was surprised to see candles everywhere. As they made their way down the aisle she realized they did give the place an atmosphere.

Ezekiel's group huddled together at the front, deep in conversation. Ezekiel saw them first and walked toward them, his hand outstretched. "Welcome, come take a seat. You know everyone here, I believe."

"Yes," Braeden said. "How are you?"

They sat, and Ezekiel took his place near the altar steps. "I want to open with a Bible reading, and then we'll pray. This is from Deuteronomy 18: 9-12."

"When you come into the land that the Lord your God is giving you, you shall not learn to follow the abominable practices of those nations. There shall not be found among you anyone who burns his son or his daughter as an offering, anyone who practices divination or tells fortunes or interprets omens, or a sorcerer or a charmer or a medium or a necromancer or one who inquires of the dead, for whoever does these things is an abomination to the Lord. And because of these abominations the Lord your God is driving them out before you."

Xantara paid little attention, until she noticed Braeden's intense look as he leaned forward, listening. What absolute rubbish. The man's a bigot. She hoped Braeden would soon tire of this!

Ezekiel's voice boomed out. "Let us pray." The group bowed their heads. "Lord, we bring before you this unfortunate woman. She has condemned her own daughter to the everlasting torment of hellfire by her failure to raise her in the knowledge of the Lord. Dear God, we know you have the power to allow her child into your kingdom, should she choose to give up her evil practices."

Xantara jumped to her feet. "You can stop right there. I'll not listen to such nonsense. Come on, Braeden, let's go."

She marched down the aisle. How dare they! She hoped they would burn in Hell. If there was such a place.

Two steps from freedom, Baxter grabbed her. Another yanked a sack over her head.

"What are you doing? Let me go this instant."

They dragged her toward the stone steps that led down to the crypt.

CHAPTER SEVEN

Today

Braeden was sickened when Ezekiel's people castrated Jonathan. Now he stepped in front of Xantara's cell door and held his arms out.

"Leave my wife alone!"

The group looked to Ezekiel for guidance, and he pointed toward the stairs. They turned as one, in silence, and moved across the crypt like a ghoulish ghost train. One by one they went up into the church. The last man doused the torches and followed them up the steps.

Xantara welcomed the darkness. As she curled into a fetal position she glimpsed a luminous figure that materialized at her left, then disappeared. A Light Being. *They're aware of my predicament.* She closed her eyes and slipped into the blessed oblivion of sleep.

Xantara felt her spirit float free. She looked down on her body, lying on the cot. She rose higher through the ceiling into the main church, then higher still until she passed the church steeple and clock. Astral travel often occurred when she was under stress, so she wasn't surprised. She usually could guide her spirit by thinking of a place, but this time she wasn't in control. She again sensed the Light Being and turned to it. It drew her upward, toward the stars, higher than she'd ever ventured before. Up and up they flew, past the moon. Earth became a small speck beneath her.

A worm hole opened before them and they hurtled through. Space and time ceased to exist. She laughed with delight as the kaleidoscope of colors whizzed by, as if she were on a roller-coaster. She forgot all her troubles as she reveled in the pleasure of the moment. Euphoria coursed through her. She felt so alive and vibrant.

They slowed as they burst out into another galaxy. Stars, planets, and moons sparkled and glowed all around her. The Light Being descended toward the planet below them. As they drew closer she marveled at the azure oceans, verdant land, and abundant vegetation that grew taller and brighter than she'd ever seen. Unbelievable colors glowed between the pockets of strange-shaped trees.

The Being led her into an enormous cavern lit by thousands of glow worms and fireflies, their lights reflected by a myriad of gems set in the walls and roof. Diamonds, rubies, emeralds and unique patterned opals were just a few that she recognized. They moved farther into the cavern until they came to a larger cave, where stalactites and stalagmites formed a cathedral-like structure which made it appear to be a throne room.

A Light Being sat on the central chair and others sat on lower seats around its base. As she stood before the throne, the Light Being who had brought her merged back with the others. She wasn't afraid. After all, they had helped heal the villagers all her life. But she was curious.

The Chief Being spoke to her telepathically. "My child, we have a problem we must solve. Over the past five thousand years you and your kind, the chosen ones born to the original families, have helped us in our mission to heal. Until now we have treated all sickness in the chosen eight families until the oldest daughter comes of age. But now your daughter is dead. She is the first novice guardian that has died before her time."

Xantara wrinkled her brow as she concentrated on the creature's words. "We have a quorum now, but then what?" she asked.

"We will reflect on that, but know this. We will help you in your current predicament. The situation will worsen, we fear, but we'll find a way. Stay open to our guidance."

Reassured, she bowed low. Her spirit returned to her body and she continued to sleep.

Braeden bent over Jonathan and put his fingers to his neck to feel for a pulse. There it was, faint, but the boy was still alive. The doctor let out a long breath. How on earth did he get involved with this? In his wildest imagination he couldn't have foreseen such brutality. How could Christians be so cruel? It was against his own moral compass, contradicted everything he stood for. He considered the time he had taken the Hippocratic Oath. With pride he'd recited the words, promising to heal, to save lives.

When his parents died he'd been a helpless child, but with his current knowledge perhaps he could have saved them. But could he, when he couldn't save his own daughter? The horror of the barbaric act he'd just witnessed dredged up old memories. Past horrors flashed through his mind.

He quietly stitched and tended Jonathan's wounds. The boy didn't stir, and that concerned him. He'd injected the area with a local but the needle's sting should have awakened him. The lad's pulse was thready, yet he was still alive. But for how long? He knew he should take the young man to the hospital, but how could he? He was a party to this, as culpable as they were. He finished and repacked his black doctor's bag.

Braeden peered through the gloom at his sleeping wife, and remorse and guilt flooded his mind. He loved her so much. How could he convince her to give up her new-age friends and accept Jesus?

The 'Fundo's,' as he had nicknamed the fundamentalists, had explained it all. Every word Ezekiel said had been like a dagger thrust into his heart. The words played through his head, again and again.

"Listen son, these are the facts. Your daughter is in pain. She writhes in agony, stuck in the deep recesses of Hell with no chance of escape. But there is a way to save her. If you and your wife accept Jesus as your Savior you'll have the opportunity to plead with God, to ask him to take her home to be with him in Heaven."

Why couldn't Xantara see the logic in that? But she continued to insist that Imogene wasn't in Hell but in another dimension, and they would someday be reunited with her.

He loved her, but at the same time he wanted her to accept his new beliefs so that their daughter could be saved. Ezekiel had promised they could change her, but now he had doubts. After the last few hours, how could he trust them? By being present, he had become implicated in their actions. Should he call the police? If he did there was no doubt he'd lose his practice and all he'd worked for.

He crept back up the steps, a broken man.

As he stepped into the nave he noticed a dark shape beside a pillar. Ezekiel! He should have known he would be there. The man was psychic!

"I've just stitched the boy up, that's all. We should get him to the hospital."

"You know we can't do that, Braeden. He'll recover, and then I'll arrange for him to go up north, back to his home town."

Ezekiel came to him. "Don't worry, God is in control. It's the right thing to do, and all your wife needs is a simple exorcism."

The man touched Braeden's shoulder and he felt a shock, as if a power went through him. He felt himself falling under the man's spell, and pulled back to break contact.

"An exorcism? What for?"

"She's controlled, made to do evil by a demon," Ezekiel said. "A simple ritual will rid her of its immoral influence, and she'll be set free."

"Are you sure?"

"Yes, it's Biblical. Jesus called out evil spirits many times. He gave us the power to do the same."

"When will you do it?"

"Soon, but I'd prefer you not to be present. You might become upset."

Braeden felt like a coward. His career would be finished if this ever got out, his life over. His mind clouded with indecision. What choice did he have? Powerful thoughts of guilt assailed him. Would an exorcism change her beliefs? He doubted it. He decided to keep quiet, let them have their way, and go home to think.

Later, as he sat in his office staring into a tumbler of whisky, thoughts tumbled in and out as if in a whirlwind. What would happen now? Would they be successful? Would they cure her?

Would they be able to release his daughter's spirit?

CHAPTER EIGHT

Xantara lay awake for hours. The oppressive darkness closed in around her, the silence absolute.

Was Jonathan alive? Could he survive such a terrible wound? She couldn't hear him breathe. Physical and mental exhaustion washed over her until at last she welcomed the oblivion of sleep.

Xantara twisted and turned, plagued with nightmares of dark shapes chasing her to a cliff edge. She screamed as they pushed her over, her heart filled with terror as she fell. Evil creatures brandished knives and axes as she lay helpless. As they fell upon her she shrieked and jerked awake.

She sensed a new energy. Something was wrong. As she opened her eyes she saw Archie and Eamon hover over her. Silently they hauled her off the bed and dragged her out of the cell, then spread-eagled her over the cold stone altar. Chains rattled as they fastened them around her wrists and secured her feet with manacles. Sharp pains radiated down her arms, the agony heightening her sense of awareness. There was no escape.

She whimpered, yanked the chains, and cringed as the kidnappers stood over her. Where was Braeden? Why didn't he help? She moved her head from side to side, but she couldn't see him. He wasn't there.

Candles perched on rock shelves in a crude circle flickered. The faces moved back and Ezekiel loomed into view, a dark scowl on his face. Horrified, she tried to figure out his intentions. Would he use the flail on her, like he did on Jonathan? She held her breath as he reached into his jacket, but to her relief he drew out a battered bible. The light flashed on a gold cross embossed into its dark leather.

The group chanted a prayer in unison:

"Our Father, which art in heaven, hallowed be thy Name. Thy Kingdom come; Thy will be done in earth, as it is in heaven. Give us this day our daily bread. And forgive us our trespasses, as we forgive them that trespass against us. And lead us not into temptation, but deliver us from evil. For thine is the kingdom, the power, and the glory, for ever and ever. Amen."

Ezekiel approached and pressed the bible against her forehead. "This is the sword of the Almighty," he said. "By its power and in the name of God the Father, Jesus the Son, and the Holy Ghost, we rebuke the demons that possess you. Be gone in the name of Jesus!"

His foul breath stank as he spat the words inches from her face. Sweat beaded and ran down her brow.

The cacophony of loud chants merging with Ezekiel's crazed rants pounded inside her head, as Ezekiel became more and more agitated. "Evil spirits, I order you to leave this woman. I command you to go, in Jesus's name." His chest swelled as he drew breath. "Go back to Hell where you belong!" He raised the Bible above his head, then jabbed it toward her. "Come out, unclean spirit." He stared at her. "What's your name?"

She didn't answer.

He pulled a large straight pin from his jacket's lapel. "This will prove you're a witch." She shrieked in pain as he repeatedly jabbed her legs and arms. Finally, he replaced the pin in his lapel, and they left.

Hours passed. Her body grew numb as her unnatural position blocked her circulation. She let her head fall back as fatigue overcame her, then was startled back to reality when icy water splashed on her chest. She looked up. Mrs. Yates dipped a pastry brush into a stone jar, as others behind her watched. The cold water showered her as she flicked the brush again and again. The woman stared at her and shook her head.

"The holy water should burn her!" someone said. "Are you sure it's been blessed?"

The woman shrugged and continued to dip and flick, dip and flick, dip and flick.

Where was Braeden? Why wasn't he here to help her, to stop this farce? She turned her face away, to avoid the splashes. Would it never end?

The group grew silent as Gloria Tierney pushed forward, pointing a large wooden cross toward her. Eamon, Gloria's husband, opened a small brass box and took communion wafers from it. He stepped to her, pinched her cheeks, and forced them into her mouth. She spluttered and spat them out.

Ezekiel leaned back, arms crossed. "See I've proved it, she is possessed!"

"Please stop," Xantara whispered.

Ezekiel recited another prayer, his voice getting higher and louder. "In the name and authority of the Lord Jesus Christ, we renounce all the powers of darkness which exist in this woman. We order all demons to leave, and go where Jesus commands you. Scuttle back to Hell where you belong."

Spittle sprayed her as he spat out each word. He eyed her, then looked up.

"In the name of Jesus Christ, I command all evil spirits to leave this woman. By the power of the Holy one, we order you to return to Hell." His face reddened and looked ready to explode. She hoped it would.

Xantara closed her eyes and withdrew into herself. The noise faded as she called upon her years of meditation practice to block them out. But the voices were too intrusive, and forced their way into her consciousness.

Ezekiel's voice squeaked and faded. He shrugged, dropped his hands to his sides, and stopped. He looked at her, then at the others.

"Why doesn't it work? She needs to repent of her sins before we can deliver her. Perhaps an incentive will help. Release her."

They unlocked the restraints and let her stagger to her feet. "Strip her," he said.

The three women tore the clothes from her until she stood before them naked. She shrank against the rock and tried to cover herself.

Ezekiel motioned to one of his members, who held a brown garment. Leather straps dangled from its sides, like belts. "Put that on her. She'll soon repent, the sinful woman."

They forced her arms through the sleeves, pulled the straps tight around her waist, and buckled them behind. Xantara clasped her arms around herself and rocked back and forth.

She didn't resist as they dragged her back and threw her down. The door clanged, and she heard the key turn. They moved away, dousing the torches as they went, until darkness descended once again. She lay there and listened as their footsteps receded. Thank goodness they were gone. She let out a breath and shuddered.

She frowned. There was something odd about the crude garment. As she rolled onto her back a burst of pain blasted through her. With horror she realized the vest was an instrument of torture. Hundreds of tiny hooks tore at her back, each movement ripping her skin. She had no option but lay still on her front. What misery!

A thin streak of red light from the first flush of sunrise pierced the vault through the air vent set high above her, and she realized how long this exorcism charade had taken. Something touched her shoulder, and she smiled. It was her daughter's hand. The emotional energy gave Imogene the power to appear, and she could sense her presence. She absorbed and renewed her strength, drawing comfort from her daughter.

Xantara blessed her gift. The ability to sense spirits first surfaced in her childhood when her father, crushed to death between a wall and a forklift the day before, appeared at the foot of her bed. She was frightened by his sudden presence, but realized he'd come to say goodbye.

Imogene's touch gave her solace, and confirmed how misguided the fundos were. Hell didn't imprison her daughter. Ezekiel and his followers were the ones who'd be shocked when they died. They were the evil souls destined to burn in Hell.

Although their prayers and accusations upset her she found security in her own beliefs, which didn't include the hellish place the radicals described. She called on the ancients to give her strength. Beings of Light, protect me. Give me courage. Deliver me from these evil people.

She needed to renew her strength before tomorrow. Comforted by the brief presence of her daughter, she fell into a deep sleep.

Several hours later she woke up. Her stomach rumbled with hunger, and her mouth seemed filled with cotton. As she sipped from the water bottle she noticed a basket covered with a bright red gingham tea-towel, which she realized belonged to Archie's wife, Ethel. The woman had carried the basket to her house many times over the past week, filled with the lightest of sponges, casseroles and pies. She was grateful for Ethel's thoughtfulness, and remembered the profusion of the woman's food stacked in her freezer. The few meals they'd eaten were delicious.

As she lifted the tea-towel, her mouth watered at the thought of a delicious meal. But instead she was greeted by stale bread and moldy cheese. Famished, she didn't care, and ate the lot. At least they didn't intend to starve her to death.

She remembered Jonathan, and tried to see him through the bars. The weak sunlight filtering in illuminated his bed. It was empty. He's gone! A lump formed in her throat, and she fought back tears. Loneliness and fresh fears rushed in, as she wondered about her own future.

She tried to contact Bryony by telepathy, as they sometimes did. She meditated to access her inner being, then concentrated hard as she sent an image of the crypt to her friend. It was useless. The trauma had quenched her power, and her thoughts bounced off the walls. She'd have to try again later.

She missed Imogene's presence and tried to recreate her touch from memory. Her heart ached as she longed for the way her life had been, trying to banish the nightmare her life had become. What did Ezekiel plan to do? When would he return?

Would Braeden come to his senses and rescue her?

CHAPTER NINE

Jonathan didn't come back. The night seemed endless, and Xantara hated the dark. She couldn't get comfortable, so she sat up. She wanted to conserve the candle but lit it anyway, to lift her spirits. As the sun rose she blew it out, grateful for the tendrils of watery sunlight. She'd lost count of time since the unfair disruption to her life, and wanted out of this never-ending nightmare.

The damp seeped into her bones, every muscle stiff with the forced inaction. Her shoulders slumped and she lay back down. Oh no, the hooks! They dug into her back, and she froze until the pain lessened. She turned over, but not before the cruel hooks did their malicious work.

As she lifted her head to try to find a comfortable position, a flash of white caught her eye through the rusted iron bars. She stood slowly and peered into the next cell. A shadowy figure lay on the cot, but it wasn't Jonathan. The figure was bulkier than the slender young man. It was obvious Jonathan was gone for good, and she hoped he was alive. But who was in his place?

She recognized the white turban. It must be Qurbani, the Sikh who ran the village store. The whites of his eyes shone. The early dawn light must have awakened him.

"Qurbani," she whispered.

"Who's there?"

"It's Xantara, the doctor's wife, from the clinic across the street."

"Why're you here? Braeden said you were at a friend's spa in Cornwall."

So, her husband had lied. She grimaced. What was wrong with him? He wasn't the man she knew so well, the one she loved.

The Sikh half sat up supported by his elbow. "Where am I, and why am I here?"

She pressed her face against the bars. "What happened?"

"Someone put a bag over my head as I left the shop. They pulled my hands behind my back, snapped on cuffs, then pushed a foul-smelling towel to my face. What is this place?"

"It's the St Michaels crypt. You know, the church on the hill behind the village."

She told him about the crazy extremists who'd kidnapped him, and recounted Jonathan's fate. Her voice broke as she relived his mutilation.

"But why am I here?" He swung his feet around and sat up.

"It's because you're a Sikh. They want to remove non-Christians, among others, from the village."

"Remove?" He gulped. "Do you mean they might kill me?"

She shook her head, then realized he couldn't see her do it. "Don't worry. They just want to scare you into leaving the village because your religion's different than theirs." She knew her voice lacked conviction.

"But I believe in God. I pray three times a day."

"Not their God, I'm afraid," she said.

Qurbani shook his head and pulled at his long, straggly beard. "Look what they did to Jonathan. What if they cut me?"

Both were silent as she pondered their fate.

"Xantara, why are you here? Are you with them?"

She smiled wryly. "No, of course not. I'm a prisoner, too. They believe my ancient beliefs and practices are sorcery."

"Then we have to get out of here."

They heard footsteps. In the near darkness she saw Eamon Tierney come down the steps. He carried a bag to her cell and shoved it through the bars. "For you." He nodded toward the Sikh. "None for the devil." He laughed and banged the bars as he left.

Qurbani stood and shook the iron door. "Hey, let me out of here! You can't keep me locked up, it's illegal!"

Eamon stomped back up the stairs. Xantara opened the bag to find more stale bread and moldy cheese, but at least the bottle of water was cold. She put it to her lips to quench her thirst, and stopped after two swallows. They allowed her just one small bottle a day, so she must conserve the precious liquid. She offered the Sikh food and water, but he refused, apparently too upset to eat.

Time passed. They talked now and then, neither in the mood for conversation. Qurbani knelt and prayed, but would his God answer him? She watched him with compassion. He was doomed. No way would they let him go. They intended to follow through on their mission, no matter what.

They both jumped as they heard the heavy studded door scrape open. Ezekiel's group chatted as they trooped down the steps, as if they were off to town for a night's entertainment. Disgusted, she folded her arms and turned her back, then glanced over her shoulder. Braeden wasn't with them. She guessed they'd realized he hadn't the stomach for "God's work." With alarm she noticed the butcher carried a cleaver in his right hand.

The same men who had chained Jonathan now dragged Qurbani out of his cell. They forced him to lie on the rock altar and secured his wrists and ankles. His scream was cut short as they forced a rag into his mouth and secured it with duct tape. Ezekiel took his place near the man's head and opened his bible.

"Idolater, son of iniquity, spawn of Satan." Spittle flew from his mouth.

Xantara banged her fist against the bars. "He's a Sikh! He believes in one God. Sikhs don't worship idols, you have it all wrong! Please, please, let him go!"

They ignored her, and she tried again.

"Can't we agree God created all men, and we all are equal and worthy of life? God must have a reason for the birth of each individual soul, a mission for each person." Her words dissipated, unheeded.

Ezekiel's face contorted with fury, and he turned to Qurbani. "Your God doesn't exist. You are destined to burn in Hell, devil worshipper. You've been judged and condemned to death. Did your God suffer as the true God did? Was your God scourged, nailed to a cross, and crucified? I think not."

Qurbani's eyes bulged as he pulled against his restraints.

Archie Redford disappeared up the stairs and returned with two wooden planks. He formed them into a cross on the stone, and the others lifted Qurbani onto them and spread his arms wide on the cross member. They nailed a block of wood beneath his feet. He looked just like Christ on the cross.

Xantara shook her cell bars. "Leave him alone, you monsters." Qurbani locked eyes with her, his terror palpable.

Eamon tied a rough blindfold around the Sikh's head as Archie retrieved a cordless drill from a bag they'd brought along. Eamon dipped into it and pulled out a hammer and a clutch of oversize nails.

Xantara pressed her face hard against the bars. She couldn't stop this barbaric brutality. She wanted to kill them, and willed her fingernails to turn into talons. If she could reach them she would tear them to pieces.

The drill whined as it bit into the Sikh's right hand. Ignoring his muffled screams, Eamon followed with his hammer, lining a nail up in the hole and banging it in. They did the same to his other hand. The smell of urine and fasces filled the room. The poor man was so frightened, he'd evacuated his bowels.

Ezekiel snapped his flail in the air and whipped the Sikh, again and again. Xantara covered her face with her hair as she sank onto the cold stone flags. When would it end? The flail's cracks went on for an eternity. At last they stopped, and she looked up.

Ezekiel nodded to Fremont Braxton.

The butcher pulled the man's long beard, stretching his head back. He swung the hatchet high and chopped down through Qurbani's neck. The axe lodged in the wood as the blood spurted out. The Punjabi's head rolled off the cross to the stone altar, held by a single strand of sinew. Braxton released the weapon, raised it again, and finished the job. The head rolled across the ground and stopped against the bars of Xantara's cell, leaving a red trail. Xantara struggled to keep the contents of her stomach down. Her knuckles whitened as she gripped the bars in fear and fury.

Part of her died with the Sikh.

The group cheered. "Thanks be to God, Father Almighty, we're your faithful servants." They dragged the body away through a curtain-covered archway she hadn't noticed before. Archie stopped to scoop up the head and dropped it into a plastic bag, like a piece of trash.

Splatters of blood covered the Fundo women's skirts and dotted their faces. So close, they'd caught the full impact of blood as it spurted out. Millicent disappeared upstairs and returned with a bucket of water. She threw the contents over the stone in an attempt to remove the blood, but it just spread more. Rivulets made their way into Xantara's space, like an overspill from the River Ganges.

The Ganges. Qurbani had told her with pride about when he was a child and his parents had taken him to visit the Holy River to watch the Hindus bathe. He said Sikhs don't believe in such pilgrimages. They look for God within their soul instead, just as Christians find the Kingdom of God within. His faith wasn't dissimilar, why wouldn't they listen? Were they so bigoted they would murder in God's name?

The group laughed and chattered as they cleaned up. The jovial atmosphere was out of place, macabre. They went back up the stairs, leaving her to contemplate the horror of her situation.

She realized now they wouldn't let her live. How could they release her, after what she'd witnessed? She sat for hours, her mind blank, staring into the distance. Inside her was a place of terror she didn't want to visit. Shock forced her mind to shut down, to protect her fragile rationality before she descended into insanity.

CHAPTER TEN

Braeden poked his head around the clinic's waiting room door and saw patients were still packed in there like pencils in a case. What was happening? There was no logical explanation for the increased sickness. He touched his own head, wishing the migraine headache would go away, and he thought of Xantara.

Many of the patients visiting his office came with old complaints. Everyone seemed to be sick. He signed the umpteenth script and looked at his watch. Lunchtime, and still more patients waited. He almost pushed Mrs. Graves out the door. As he reached to press the bell to signal the next patient, old Mr. Fisher with his arthritic hip, to come in, the door swung open and his mother-in-law waltzed in with a determined expression. She appeared ready to do battle.

"Sabina, how are you?"

"Where is Xantara?" She drew in a breath. "What's all this nonsense about friends in Cornwall? She's never mentioned any such friends to me. I've called her cell phone numerous times, and no answer."

Braeden hesitated. He couldn't handle this whole mess for much longer, but knew he had no choice but to continue the charade.

"Look, don't worry. I've spoken to her, and she'll be back next week. An old college friend heard about Imogene and invited her to stay at her spa near Chiverton Cross as long as she liked. Xantara needed a change of scenery, and I encouraged her to go."

She eyed him carefully. "What's the name of this spa?"

"I can't recall, but don't worry. She needs space. Be patient, she'll be home soon."

Sabina seemed mollified, although still suspicious. He was thankful he'd never given her reason to doubt him. She chatted about her grandson Alistair for a while, then stood.

"Next time you talk to her, please tell her to call me." She leant over the desk and pecked his cheek. "Look after yourself, you look exhausted."

The door closed behind her, and Braeden shrunk down in his chair. His head dropped into his hands. What could he do? Ezekiel's explanations seemed so right. He wanted to save Xantara and Imogene, but his daughter came first. He couldn't leave her in Hell, could he? Yes, his motives were pure, but life was unfair. How could he fix this mess?

His head still ached, and a busy afternoon of house calls lay ahead. Braeden swallowed two pain-killers, picked up his case, and headed out to his lime-green Renault. The six house calls took all afternoon. The last patient waved to him as he climbed into his car.

He decided to confront Ezekiel. The man would release his wife or he would go to the police, even if it cost him his career. The engine revved as he backed out and pointed toward the rectory. Minutes later he pressed the brass bell. The door opened immediately, and Millicent ushered him into the drawing room.

"Take a seat, dear. I'll tell Ezekiel you're here."

Braeden couldn't sit still. He wandered over to the large bay window and looked out over the impressive driveway. His heart throbbed, and a painful lump formed in his throat. He couldn't take much more.

Ezekiel strode into the room. "Good to see you, boy." He held out his hand. Braeden hesitated, then shook it. "Sit down. Millie will bring you tea and a piece of her delicious fruitcake."

Braeden sat in a high-backed armchair and Ezekiel took a seat opposite him, a wide grin on his face. Braeden stared back. Didn't the man worry he'd be found out? How could he just sit there, so relaxed?

"How's Jonathan?" Braeden asked. After Ezekiel found out he'd stitched Jonathan's wounds, he'd banned him from the crypt.

"Fine, boy, just fine. We warned him off, and he went back up north to his home town. I own the building his shop was in, and cancelled the lease. No problems there."

"Won't he tell the police what happened?"

"No, no—I told him we'd hunt him down and kill him if he as much as hinted to anybody."

Braeden raised his eyebrows, but said nothing. He'd been so blind. Ezekiel was insane, and only God knew what he might do next. Why didn't he see that before? He must rescue Xantara, and soon.

"About Xantara. I think…"

Millicent bustled in to set the table. "Would you like cream on your cake?"

"No, thank you." He was sick to his stomach, but drained the teacup in one gulp. He looked back at Ezekiel. "Did you perform the exorcism?"

Ezekiel shifted in his chair and picked imaginary lint off his jacket. "It didn't work. The demons wouldn't leave her, but we did weaken them. I plan a final session."

"Look, Ezekiel, I want Xantara freed now. Let me convince her, I'm sure I can. She's learned her lesson and will be ready to listen."

"Relax just a couple more days." Ezekiel leant forward. "I want to perform another exorcism, a more powerful one. It's the right decision, to cast the devils out. I promise you, when her mind is free from them she'll accept our beliefs."

Braeden shook his head and cracked his fingers, each click a miniature explosion. "You swear she can come back home, then? Her mother visited the clinic today. I can't put her off much longer."

"I promise you, it'll work out. The Lord told me what to do. What more could you ask?"

Braeden drained his second cup of tea and stood. "So, when will you do it?"

"Son, don't worry about it."

"I want to be there, in case she needs me." He knew his voice sounded like a child begging his father for a treat.

"You might get upset, and you've been through enough," Ezekiel said, looking concerned. His smile seemed forced. "She'll be home before you know it, and will have forgotten all this New Age nonsense." Ezekiel grasped Braeden's arm and steered him toward the door.

Braeden drove home and parked. He sat in his car, his brow furrowed. He had to rescue her! The man was a psychopath, manipulative and without a conscience. And he'd kidnapped his wife. Enough! He'd get help, whatever the cost.

A slow anger burned in his stomach. He gunned the engine and sped off toward the church. He would get her, beg her forgiveness. What a fool he'd been!

Braeden reached the church, and saw the parking lot was empty. He jumped out and ran to the door. Unlocked, thank God. He stepped inside and bolted it behind him. The brilliant display of leaded windows highlighted the dark interior, depicting scenes from the Sermon on the Mount. He marched down the aisle toward the door behind the vestry.

Black velvet drapes hanging from brass hoops concealed the entrance. He drew them back and turned the knob. Locked! Of course they would lock it. He pounded the solid oak door, shouting her name, until his hands hurt.

Where was the key?

He rummaged under the altar, searched the vestry, looked everywhere, but couldn't find it. He pushed his hair back and sank down on the altar steps. What now? He should go to the police, or the pastor. Or perhaps he should wait to see if the second exorcism worked.

He would give them three more days, and that's all.

Chapter Eleven

The chaplain kept a wary eye on Henry Wall as he moved away from him to pick up his prayer book. It would be a mistake to turn his back. The man's expressionless eyes followed him like lasers. He sat, opened his book, and looked across the table.

"So you'd like to know more about God?"

His chair's front legs lifted as the prisoner leaned back. He turned his hands palms up. "I'm sorry about what I've done, and I want to make amends."

The chaplain pushed his sleeves up and tugged at his stiff white collar. The man was a lunatic. Even God couldn't forgive him, not after he smashed a two-month-old baby against a wall to make a point. Then he'd raped the mother and slashed her throat until her head was almost severed. This whole "got religion" thing was a charade, a ploy for the parole board.

"I hear you have a parole review next month."

Henry gestured again, his arms open. "I know what you're thinking, but the kid and her mother deserved it. I was a teenager then. Can't you understand?"

"No, I can't. You don't sound remorseful at all." The chaplain leaned away.

Henry's face darkened. "Look, vicar. I want you to tell the board I'm a changed man. I'm now a Christian, and I deserve a chance."

"I'm sorry, but in all good conscience, I can't." He flinched as the prisoner stood, and moved his chair back a couple inches.

"You should have listened, old man! You piece of shit. Now you can meet your maker ahead of time." The prisoner's chair materialized above the chaplain, and crashed down on his defenseless head. He knew no more.

Detective McCullage glanced out his window, and smiled. What a pleasant day. He looked back at the pile of office reports stacked before him and shook his head.

His phone trilled, and he picked it up. "Yes, can I help you?"

"Constable Higgins, sir. I cover the villages south of Swindon."

"Yes?"

"Two people have disappeared from Monkton St Michael under suspicious circumstances. Villagers say two High Street shops—a beauty shop and a grocery—have closed without cause."

McCullage frowned. "Shops close all the time."

"Yeah, I suppose. But the hairdresser and the grocer—Jonathan Matthews and Qurbani Singh—haven't been seen since."

Jim McCullage mentally shrugged. Why would anyone want to live in such an isolated place, anyhow? But the excuse to leave the office was irresistible, the glorious day beckoned.

"Give me the details and I'll investigate."

He scribbled in his notebook, thanked the caller, and left the office. His step lightened, and he smiled. The drive through the villages would be pleasant.

His cell phone rang, and he answered. There'd been a murder at Erlestoke prison, which lay between Devizes and Westbury. He'd go there first, and stop in Monkton St Michael on his return.

He reached Erlestoke Manor House and Estate, now government owned, which housed the new prison building. Its beautiful surrounds were wasted on the unappreciative scum who lived there. Typical of government. Too much money and political correctness.

He gave his keys and phone to a receptionist and waited for an escort. A dour-faced warden arrived and led him to the chaplaincy, where a body of a man sprawled across the floor. His head was bludgeoned and part of his brain lay exposed like a pale grey egg in a nest. A chair lay broken in two and covered in blood.

The warden stepped back to allow the detective a clear view. "Bloody maniac. Henry Wall did it. He belongs in Dartmoor, if you ask me."

"Lock the room down," McCullage said. "The forensics team will come by later. Gruesome murder, but at least it was quick. I agree Wall should be in Dartmoor. God knows why the judge sent him here."

They left the room, and he waited while the warden locked the door. "I'd like to talk to him now, please."

"This way sir, follow me."

The warden led him down several long grey corridors to a locked interview room. He searched his ring of keys for the right one. "I'll leave you to it, then. It's quite safe, he's shackled."

They entered the room, which held a steel table and two chairs, all bolted down. Henry sat in one, looking bored.

The warden left and McCullage sat across from him and pulled out his notebook. High up, a camera blinked. The meeting was being recorded and he'd pull the footage later.

"Why did you do it?"

The convict sneered. "Why not? He deserved it."

"Go on."

"He should have done what I asked. If you think about it, I did him a favor. Now he's with his God." He drew his sleeve across his nose and inspected the deposit. "Look, can we finish up here?"

McCullage was well-read on psychopathic traits, and here before him was a real live example. This was a waste of his time. The man had no remorse, and had found a way to justify his actions. Why the system didn't lock these people up in a lead-lined airtight box, he didn't know. The problem was, half the establishment was run by psychopaths.

Over the next two hours the man refused to answer questions, and McCullage gave up. He would resume the interrogation the next day.

McCullage parked, and eyed the two shops before him. Their blinds were drawn, and obviously they were closed. He turned to the next one, a butcher shop. He'd start there.

He entered the shop and the butcher looked up from behind the counter, all smiles, wiping his bloody hands on an already soiled white apron. McCullage stared at it. It seemed a good incentive to become a vegetarian, and perhaps he would.

"Good morning." he said.

The butcher held out his hand, and McCullage ignored it.

"How can I help you, sir? Our tenderloins are especially tender today."

McCullage shielded his eyes from the sun coming through the window. "The hairdresser and grocer next door have left, without a word to their customers. Do you know why?"

"Outsiders," he said. "I've heard they found the place too small, and made no money. Ezekiel Yates owns both properties, maybe he can tell you more." He pointed across the street. "That's his place, above the post office. He's a solicitor."

"Thanks."

The butcher gave him a cheery wave as he stepped outside the shop.

McCullage crossed the street and pushed the brass bell, and heard the buzzer announce his arrival upstairs. The door was open, so he entered and climbed the polished wood stairs, past framed legal-looking certificates on the magnolia walls. He counted nine. As he reached the top a wire-spectacled middle-aged woman stood up from her desk.

"Can I help you?"

"Ezekiel Yates. Is he here?"

"Wait here—I'll see if he's available."

She vanished through a polished oak door and he sat, and soon was tapping his knee, hoping she wouldn't be long. After ten minutes, she reappeared.

"Mr. Yates will see you now. This way, please."

He followed her into the lawyer's office. A man stood and extended his hand, and the detective shook it. "Beautiful weather, isn't it? Please take a seat and tell me how I may help you."

He motioned McCullage to a maroon leather regency style chair, its padding held in place with uncomfortable brass studs. He sat upright to avoid the hard back. Yates leaned back and clasped his hands behind his head. An old trick, McCullage thought. Intimidation wouldn't work with him.

The detective took his time. As Ezekiel confirmed he owned both properties, he realized he didn't like the lawyer and couldn't trust him. Why, he wasn't sure.

"Jonathan begged me to release him from his contract," Ezekiel said. "There wasn't enough business, and he couldn't afford to stay. Said he missed his family up in Sheffield. I felt sorry for the young lad and cancelled his lease."

McCullage pulled out his notebook and pen, licked his finger, and flicked it open. "His new address?"

"Sorry, he wasn't sure which family member he would stay with. He promised to let me know later."

McCullage gave him his business card. "Please, email it to me. Where is Qurbani Singh, the grocer?"

The lawyer hesitated, but soon recovered control.

"Singh. Nice chap, gone back to India. He wants to arrange for his family to join him in England, said it could take a few months. Damned inconvenient for the village, I must say. We have to drive to Avebury now, just for a bottle of milk or loaf of bread."

Detective McCullage thanked him, shook his hand again, and hurried back to his car. The drive had been pleasant, but he hankered for civilization. He mulled over the day's events as he navigated the narrow lanes hemmed in by overgrown hedgerows. It was strange for two shops to shut within days of each other, but the explanations were plausible.

He couldn't pin down why, but Yates seemed to be a slimy character. He trusted his instincts, though, and resolved to keep him in mind.

He switched his thoughts to a pint of ale, chicken, and chips at the Cock-and-Bull in Swindon, and pressed the accelerator harder.

Chapter Twelve

Ezekiel thought of the now-defunct secret government underground city in Burlington, near Corsham, as he drove toward it to visit his cousin, Obadiah Yates.

The British public wasn't aware of this vast subterranean metropolis before its recent decommission. It was built in the late nineteen fifties to protect the prime minister, his cabinet, and almost four thousand civil servants from a possible nuclear war. Obadiah, Officer-in-Charge, had organized and managed its various departments, offices, hospital, supplies, stores, and even a telephone exchange. The Ministry of Defense closed it ten years before, and retired him. All the hidden entrances were blocked with concrete to prevent vandalism.

When it closed, Obadiah used his special knowledge of the place to convert it to his and Ezekiel's own purposes. It was a God-send, because it generated a handsome income to fund their cause.

Ezekiel parked his silver Jaguar near the converted mill Obadiah lived in and sat for a moment, a distant, unfocused smile on his face. The waterwheel still turned, and he watched it splash water into the stream. The mechanical action soothed his soul. He got out and approached the building, looked at his Omega Sea-master watch, and lifted the mill's knocker. He prided himself as always being on time. Never late, never early.

The door opened, and Obadiah appeared. "Welcome Brother," he said, extending his hand. Ezekiel shook it, then followed him through the west wing into the study. He settled into an overstuffed, red leather chair, and watched his cousin pour two glasses of vintage port from a

Waterford crystal decanter. Obadiah handed one glass to Ezekiel, and raised his own glass. "To our success," he said.

Ezekiel clinked glasses with his cousin. "Hear, hear. What progress have you made this month?"

"We've taken five blasphemers off the street. Hard to re-educate them, I must say, so a couple are still locked up."

Ezekiel sipped his wine. "Did anyone see you?"

"I don't think so. We kept our faces covered, and dropped them off in Swindon when we finished." Obadiah laughed. "We do our best to persuade them to change."

"Good man."

Ezekiel told his cousin about his own group's progress, but didn't mention the deaths. Obadiah wouldn't like it.

His cousin paused, and rubbed his chin. "Do you think we should lay low for a while? Some have filed complaints with the police, but their stories sound so fantastic they aren't believed."

"What did my father tell us on his deathbed?" Ezekiel's mind drifted back to his childhood. His father raised him and his three orphaned cousins, including Obadiah. Harsh discipline and indoctrination had shaped their childhood.

His cousin looked down at his glass. "He told us to complete the great commission," he said, softly. "To cleanse the world, one evil soul at a time."

"That's right. Well, it's time to go. I have calls to make in Swindon." He said a brief prayer of thanks and left.

Obadiah relaxed into his captain's chair, sipped the rest of his drink, and ran his hand through his military style crew cut. How much longer could they get away with it? Too many people kidnapped in a short time, it was dangerous. True, he blindfolded them and dropped them back at the spot they'd been taken from. But the time in-between wasn't pleasant, and some had now reported the mistreatment. He closed his eyes and breathed deeply. He didn't want to end up in prison. But he so enjoyed it!

He decided to visit the detainees to see if he could hasten their confession and rehabilitation. The underground city was perfect, a no-brainer, and he knew every inch.

Obadiah opened the garage. He drove a classic green Bentley with leather seats and impeccable paintwork. He'd resisted the burden of a wife, as he much preferred to indulge his passions. The Bentley's restoration had taken years, but was worth the time and cost. He loved the old girl.

He rubbed a smudge off the bonnet with his handkerchief and opened the door. He hated to drive the beauty along the dirt track that led to the tunnel a few miles from home, but the rough road suited his purposes. The track ended at a copse of beech trees, the ideal place for a private entrance to his underground playground.

A few yards in he cleared fallen branches away to expose a battered, camouflaged trapdoor. He pulled the iron ring and lifted it to reveal steel rungs, which faded from view as the daylight petered out after a few feet. He stepped down, clicked on his flashlight, and pulled the hatch shut behind him.

He descended fifteen feet down the ladder to a concrete-lined tunnel. He clicked the wall switch and the bulkhead lights flickered on. Walking the passageway, a mile in length, counted as his exercise for the day. He liked to stay healthy and didn't mind the long trek into the city proper.

He strode out, careful to avoid contact with the side walls. Obadiah cared about his clothes. His tweed jacket topped tan slacks and framed a crisp white shirt and dark blue silk tie. The Italian silk, one of many, sported a subtle paisley pattern. Tall and fit, he enjoyed the walk. Unlike Ezekiel he had no woman to fatten him up. He was proud of his flat stomach and broad chest. He stroked the smooth tie.

He entered the industrial kitchen and opened the fridge. Dry after the exercise, he quaffed a bottle of water. He pulled out several more bottles and a bag of biscuits to feed the prisoners.

He was pleased he could house them in an actual prison. The facility's original plan, modeled after the Westgate prison in London, included a cell block to hold any dissidents in case of attack. Its two levels connected with steel steps and bridges. Each solid steel cell door included a small window to view the occupants. Food was passed through a slot underneath it.

When the five prisoners, held in separate cells, heard him, they yelled. Their shouts reminded him of a soccer game, the first and last he'd ever attended. He went down the passageway shoving a water bottle and a few of biscuits through each slot, leaving them open so they could hear him clearly.

"Are you ready to accept Jesus?"

He stumbled back as they yelled "No!" in unison, cursing and threatening to hang, draw and quarter him when they got out.

Obadiah raised his voice. "If you want me to let you out, you'll have to renounce your evil ways and accept Jesus into your hearts. Listen up, sinners. You'll stay locked up until you do."

The response was another round of blasphemous shouts. He decided to return later, with reinforcements. Stronger tactics and added muscle were needed.

"I'll be back, and you'll be sorry."

Obadiah decided to check their commercial enterprises. He mounted a Segway and the machine purred off toward the northern block. He enjoyed the two-wheeled vehicle, which made the vast network of underground roads, sixty miles of them, manageable. Pity the machine's height precluded its use in the entry tunnel.

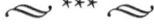

Obadiah's band of disciples met in the beech wood that evening at ten o'clock. They were a questionable lot—nine people aged eighteen to eighty—but they were the best he could get. They included the Freemans, a complete family of mother, father and two teenage sons. Standing next to them were Bert and Alice Weaver, in their mid-fifties and as nasty as they come. Two single men, Joseph and Noah, both in their forties, completed the group.

They switched on powerful flashlights, descended the shaft and an hour later arrived at the prison. Obadiah signaled them to cover their faces, and they donned black ski masks with eye and mouth cut-outs.

Obadiah unlocked the first cell and motioned the two younger men to fetch the prisoner, a young drug addict. He struggled to break free, but was no match for two grown men. They marched him to the kitchen, tied him face up onto the wide stainless steel preparation table, and waited for further instructions.

Obadiah licked his lips. "Strip off his shirt."

He stared at the tattoos that covered the boy's arms. Disgusted, he inspected the evil icons, devils with horns, skulls, and obscene words. A whimsical love heart with the word "Mom" was tattooed on his shoulder. The boy looked up in defiance and spat into their faces.

Mrs. Freeman switched the stove's gas on and held a metal rod in the flames, and they all watched it change from black to a dull red glow. She turned up the heat, and the flames licked the rod until they blazed with bright crimson and yellow hues. She handed it to Obadiah.

The boy's eyes bulged with horror as the implement of torture came into view. Before he could make a sound the bar sizzled against a horned devil face on his chest. The smell of burned flesh reached their nostrils as small puffs of grey smoke rose like signals from a Red Indian's fire. The older couple covered their ears as tortured cries tore through the room, as they burned off every tattoo.

Obadiah leaned in close to the youth's ear. "You shall not make any cuts on your body for the dead or tattoo yourselves: I am the Lord. Leviticus 19:28." He smiled, watching the youth pass out from the unbearable pain.

The group decided to call it a night. Mr. Freeman fetched a stretcher from the army stores, and they carried the unconscious boy back through the tunnel. They threw him onto a farm truck's open bed and drove back to town. After midnight, in a quiet Swindon backstreet, they rolled the unconscious boy onto the pavement.

They would hunt again.

Chapter Thirteen

Jim McCullage sat at his desk in the Swindon police constabulary annex, fingering a recent award for bravery he used as a paperweight. Dick Tracey comics and Sherlock Holmes adventures had fueled his ambition when he was a child, and he had decided to become a detective then. He joined the force when he was eighteen and now, at forty-seven, he was as keen as ever to solve crimes.

He laid his paperweight aside and glanced about his office. Papers stacked high suggested a certain carelessness. Others in the department had commented about the mess over the years, but he could find anything he wanted, so ignored the clutter, and them. His desk had seen better days and the rickety black chair sagged under his solid build, but that wasn't his fault.

He tilted his head to one side and again studied the file he held, the quarter's list of reported crime. Why were the complaints forty per cent higher than the previous quarter?

An unusual assault on a teenager caught his attention. The youth suffered burns over his chest and arms, inflicted by unknown persons, and was still in hospital. He punched a reference number on his keyboard and retrieved the details, and frowned. He knew the teen, in trouble since the age of twelve. His list of offences included shoplifting and drug abuse, and now they'd escalated to aggravated burglary.

A month before, the boy had knocked over a pensioner as he snatched her purse, but the incident received minimal investigation. The sergeant had consigned the case to a junior, apparently believing the boy had gotten what he deserved.

Jim sipped his sweet strong black coffee as he reread the case's details. They were unusual. His tattoos had been burned off with a poker, and his earrings had been torn out. Doctors stitched both lobes, and the boy was still undergoing skin grafts.

Jim decided to pay him a visit.

The kid lay in bed swathed with bandages, looking dejected and docile. Jim had never seen him so quiet, his spark quenched. He pulled up a green vinyl chair and sat down as he studied the boy. The kid turned his head away as soon as he recognized the detective.

McCullage sat a moment, stretched his arms, and relaxed. "Fantastic game Saturday."

The boy lay still, staring at the wall.

"Who'd have guessed it, Swindon beating the champions? The Devizes football team must be crying in their beers. What a landslide! Did you watch it?"

The boy half-turned toward him.

"The center-forward, what's his name? Bugsy, that's it. What a shot! The decisive goal right before the whistle. Who'd have thought our team would beat the county champions?"

The boy perked up and made eye contact. At last he had his full attention. He soon established the youth had no idea who had taken him, or where. They had put a hood on him, then bundled him into the boot of a car. The boy estimated the journey had lasted about twenty minutes.

The abductors made him climb down a metal-runged ladder, then walk for ages, about an hour, he guessed, then pushed him into a cell. He heard shouts from other people, but didn't know where they came from. A man's voice shouted at him to repent of his sins and become a Christian. A couple of days passed before they gave him food and water.

Later they dragged him into a kitchen and strapped him to a table and burned him.

The boy flinched at the memory. "It was horrible. I believed they'd kill me."

Jim felt sorry for him. "How many people were involved?"

"I'd say eight or nine."

"Could you identify them?"

The boy frowned, thinking. "No, they all wore hoods with holes cut out for their eyes."

"What happened next?"

"I dunno. I passed out and woke up by my house. It was late, and Ma wasn't pleased, I got her out of bed. She called the ambulance."

Jim scribbled in his notebook. "Can you give me any more details? Maybe about where they took you?"

"I was too scared to look, but I did notice the kitchen was big. Like the one at the cricket pavilion."

"Thanks kid, I'll do my best to find out who did this to you. Get well soon."

Jim mulled it over and went through possible perpetrators. Maybe a local outlaw motorcycle gang did it. He quickly discarded that possibility, since the boy mentioned a man who shouted about God and evil. He decided to look through the other complaints and see if he could find a similar report.

Jim headed for the office. He stopped to buy a filled roll for lunch, and munched it at his desk as he studied the two lists. He noticed another boy about the same age was snatched in a similar fashion. He was a druggie too, but didn't remember much, as he suffered the pangs of heroin withdrawal during the incident. An officer found him and took him to rehab, where he remained.

Jim checked the year's crime figures, and a pattern emerged. Eight abduction cases were reported, within a two-month period. One prostitute found dumped in a gutter had been locked into an old iron chastity belt. She had no idea who did it, or why. Similar stories came to light, and Jim became determined to find the perpetrators.

The next day a woman knocked on his office door.

"I'm Helen," she said. "Someone kidnapped me, and the desk sergeant sent me to see you."

"Come in." He pointed to a chair. "Tell me about it."

She sat, and put her large purse in her lap. Unremarkable in looks, she carried a few extra pounds around her middle. Her permed hair hung down in fuzzy tendrils around a plump but pleasant face. A black lacy shawl covered a purple and gold patterned skirt.

"I'm a medium and Tarot card reader," she said. "I tell people their fortunes, and contact deceased loved ones. Sometimes I help young women discover the identity of their future husbands."

McCullage frowned. "And what's that got to do with your abduction?"

She shrugged. "I think my work's the reason they targeted me."

His preferred drawing out a victim's statement with patience, since he'd found it the most efficient way to extract the smallest details. He waited in silence for her to collect her thoughts.

"A man phoned to make an appointment for a reading," she said. "I made him one for two o'clock Saturday afternoon, six days ago. When I opened the door, he forced himself inside. He wore a ski mask."

Her voice wavered, and she looked distressed.

"Take your time. What did he do?"

"He twisted my arm behind me and held a knife to my throat." She looked frightened as she recalled the terror. "He forced me to sit in a chair and placed a bag over my head, then tied me up."

"And then?"

"I heard a motor, the garage door. Then I heard a car. Later, I realized he'd backed it in."

McCullage stepped to the cooler, drew a paper cup of water, and handed it to her. "What happened next?"

She sipped it. "It was horrible. He forced me into the car boot, and slammed it shut. I was afraid I'd suffocate. We drove off, and about twenty minutes later he told me to get out. He half carried me down some steps, then made me walk for ages."

The same story as the druggie, Jim realized. "Where do you think you were?"

She again sipped her water. "I think underground, the air smelt dank."

"What else can you remember? Take your time."

"He pushed me," she said. "I heard a door slam. After a while I took the hood off and saw I was in a concrete room with a steel door. Much later someone pushed a water bottle and biscuits through a slot."

McCullage tapped his pen. "Then?"

"A man's voice told me to repent. He said if I didn't, I'd burn in hell and be damned forever. He ranted that fortune-tellers were damned by God. After a while I told him I repented, and was sorry and would follow God. I guess he didn't believe me, though, because this same conversation happened for days."

"How did you get out?"

"Eventually, he said he believed me, and pushed the hood through the door slot. I put it on and he guided me back. They put me into the car boot again, and let me out on the outskirts of town."

"What make of car?" Jim asked.

"I don't know. He told me to leave the hood on and sit on the grass verge for half an hour. I'm sorry, but that's all I can tell you." She gave her name and address and thanked him.

"I'll check it out," he said.

He saw her out. At least she hadn't been hurt. Mediums and Tarot readers lived in a different world than his, but she seemed pleasant enough, and he felt sorry for her traumatic experience. This extra information strengthened his determination to solve these cases.

He played with his paperweight again. Were the disappearances in Monkton St Michael connected to these cases? He worked through them in his mind. His gut feeling was that they were linked.

Chapter Fourteen

Helen cowered from the demonic faces that loomed over her. A tall tower stood beside her, and as she looked up, rocks reigned down. Stones crushed her body like a spoon against an eggshell, cutting and tearing her skin.

She jerked awake, screaming. The bed sheet was wrapped around her like a mummy. She must have tossed and turned like a ship in a cyclone. Sweat poured down her face as she gulped air to release her from the dream. She switched on the bedside lamp and struggled to compose herself.

Spirit had a message for her, and the nightmare would be repeated until she deciphered it. She sipped water and lay back, looking at the ceiling. What did it mean?

 ***

The next day the doorbell rang, and Helen opened it to see Sybil, there for her afternoon tarot reading appointment. They met when Helen had joined the Swindon Spiritualist Church years before, hoping to communicate with her late husband through the resident medium. The spiritualist community soon discovered her own ability and helped her develop it. Within months she became a frequent speaker and medium herself.

Sybil sat at the table, and Helen bowed her head in meditation. She looked up and smiled. "How are you, Sybil?"

"Not well. Sabina's anxious," she said. "Xantara has been missing for days. She's supposed to be with a friend in Cornwall, but she hasn't heard from her and she's worried."

Imogene's unexpected death had been dreadful, and Helen's heart ached for her friend. "Well, let's see what the cards tell us."

She opened the purple satin cloth to reveal her distinctive Tarot pack, caressed the well-worn cards, and placed them in front of Sybil. "Please cut the pack into three." She dealt the cards, face down, to form a Celtic cross.

Helen turned over the first card, and her eyes widened. The Tower. Then it came to her. Spirit now confirmed her dream had been concerned with Imogene's death. "Look, Sybil. The card shows a tower struck in two by lightning, with rocks falling from it."

Sybil touched the card and a tear slid down her face. "Poor Imogene, how I miss her. Is it a sign? What does the card mean?"

"It shows an event which will destroy perceived happiness. The bolt of lightning tells us to expect an unforeseen and unpleasant experience. It's a card of misfortune."

"But the event has already happened, hasn't it?"

Helen stared down at the card. "I'm sorry, but it speaks of another incident. Let's see what the other cards say."

She turned the next card, Justice. "There may be more behind the death of your great-niece. Was it an accident? This card means truth will be revealed, and justice will prevail." She frowned, studying it closely. "I see an element of Karma. If someone is behind her death either in a physical or spiritual sense, the culprit will die in a similar fashion."

Helen turned the third card, smiled, and looked up. "The High Priestess. She symbolizes the obscurities of life and unveils mysteries. She reveals truth to inquirers, but first they have to travel through the veil. To do this you must meditate and interpret your dreams."

Helen described her dream to Sybil. "I think it's related to Imogene," she said. "Keep notes of your dreams, and ideas may arise when you meditate. We'll find the truth."

She returned the Tarot cards to their satin-cloth home with reverence, handling them with care to protect the power they held.

Helen saw concern on Sybil's face. "Let's try to contact Imogene." She lit several candles and drew the dark velvet curtains, since a peaceful atmosphere was essential to attract the spirits. Helen took Sybil's hands across the table and closed her eyes. In her mind, she called out to her spirit guide. Eugene answered.

"I ask you to bring forth the spirit of Imogene."

Helen opened her eyes and noticed a slight movement behind Sybil. A shadowy form swirled, then coalesced into a pale image of a young girl. She caught her breath and sat still. It was Imogene.

Telepathic messages flowed between them. The pictures weren't clear, but the tower and the rocks looked the same as in her dream. A parchment materialized, and words written by an unseen hand appeared. Help Mommy. The image faded, and she was gone.

She relayed this to Sybil, who looked puzzled. "Why would Xantara need help? She's in Cornwall at the moment. But of course I'll help her in any way I can."

Helen shook her head. "This is a profound message. I'm sorry, but Xantara must be in trouble."

Sybil tapped her index finger on her lip. "I can't imagine what could be wrong. I'll phone her mother when I get home."

Helen opened the curtains and blew out the candles. "Please let me know if I can help, and call me right away if you have any news of Xantara." She hugged her, and walked her to the front door.

Sybil walked along the road toward home. Why would Xantara need help? What could it be, if not an accident? She'd telephone her twin as soon as possible. It's the worst pain imaginable to lose a child or grandchild, and she would support her sister and niece with her last breath. The familiar ache of loss cramped her stomach. A loss of her own she'd never shared with her family. At the time, she'd had no choice but to endure it alone.

She thought back to many years earlier, to their eighteenth birthday, a day when she and her twin were consumed with excitement. Tonight her sister Sabina would take her rightful place as a Guardian. If she had been born first...well, she wasn't. She loved her sister, and it pleased her to dress her in the ceremonial robes.

Near midnight, she accompanied her mother and twin to the circle of stones, which stood stark against the night sky. A full harvest moon traced a silvery path along the grass and over the keystone. The others were there, and she heard the tinkle of tambourines and the drums' soft beat. Her heart swelled with anticipation.

She stood well back to watch the ceremony, aware her presence was a privilege. Sabina looked glorious. Her face glowed as she took her solemn vows.

As she watched, a hand clasped over her mouth from behind. She struggled, but her assailant was strong, and pulled her backwards into the shadows behind a huge rock. The man wore dark clothes and a black ski mask. Hand over her mouth, he lifted her dress and brutally raped her, then squeezed her neck until she passed out.

She came to as she heard her mother call, and smoothed her dress as she stood. Her knees trembled, and she wanted to wash the filth from her body. "I'm...here, Mom." She wanted to run and never stop, but she couldn't spoil this historic night. "Wasn't...wasn't it wonderful?" The three women linked arms and strolled back to their cottage.

She lay in bed and replayed the violation. The tape played all night, until she fell asleep as the morning sun found a chink in the curtain. Later she got out of bed and ran a bath. She soaked for a long time. Should she tell? Her mother would be horrified, and the neighbors— well... a baby born out of wedlock was inconceivable. She hoped it would go away. Her lip quivered, and she wept.

Months passed, and she was pregnant, with no idea of the father's identity. She'd always confided in her sister, but each time she tried now, shame overcame her. A solution arrived in the form of a letter from her attacker. He said that, if a pregnancy had resulted, she could pick up a parcel left under a nearby hedgerow and follow the directions within.

She ran along the lane and searched under the hedge, and her hand touched the brown paper parcel. She untied its string and ripped off the paper. Money, and a letter! She counted the five-pound notes. One hundred pounds, it was a fortune. She sat on the grass and opened the letter. It contained instructions for her to go to a home for unwed mothers.

She would do it. A Heaven-sent solution, and no one need ever know. The next day she surprised her mother and sister when she told them she had secured a nanny job, up north. She hated the necessity to be devious. It wasn't her nature, but had to be done.

Pain shot through her as she pushed. The nurse appeared distant and pursed her lips each time she let out a cry. Perspiration covered her forehead, and she longed for her mother and sister. At last the head crowned, and she pushed harder. The baby emerged.

The contract allowed her an hour with her son before the adoption. She inspected him all over. A perfect child lay in her arms, except for the obvious fact of his albinism. This genetic condition didn't surprise her, but when she looked into his eyes she recoiled. They were soulless, empty, a ghost child. How strange! She shuddered. Perhaps adoption was the wisest option. The nurse returned, and she handed him over.

Would she ever see him again?

Chapter Fifteen

Ezekiel climbed two sets of stairs toward the attic and entered his prayer closet. The room, abandoned for the last sixty years until he converted it, had once housed the rectory servant.

A solid wooden cross hung above a window. The servant's rusted cast iron bed still stood against the wall, with a charcoal and white ticking mattress, thick with dust, as if it awaited her return. The davenport desk sat against the west wall, another cross flanked by two brass candlesticks on its top.

He locked the door behind him and lit the candles, then knelt on a silk cushion he'd purloined from the drawing room.

He treasured his sanctuary. Millicent would never dare enter his prayer closet, whether he was at home or not. He liked to come up at first light, when the pale sun added atmosphere. Head in hands, he waited on his Lord and Savior.

He opened his Bible and read the marked verses:

This son of ours is stubborn and rebellious. He will not obey us. He is a profligate and a drunkard. Then all the men of his town shall stone him to death.

Keeping steadfast love for thousands, forgiving iniquity and transgression and sin, but who will by no means clear the guilty, visiting the iniquity of the fathers on the children and the children's children, to the third and the fourth generation.

God's message was clear. Children had to pay for their parents' sins, right down to the third generation. The girl's death by stoning fit in with His commandments. The Lord had determined the time and place to fulfill the scripture.

He closed his eyes, bowed, and thought about the momentous day, many years before, when God had appeared and selected him to do his bidding. He was nine years old, and his father had hauled him up the stairs by his ear. He'd crunched up his face in an effort not to cry, for the slightest whimper would have guaranteed a harder beating. His father pushed him into the bedroom and he landed in a heap, bruised by hard, bare boards.

"Read the devil's work, would you?" he said.

"A comic, Father, that's all."

He flinched as his father clouted him around his head. "You know what to do."

Ezekiel got up, pulled off his trousers and underpants, and lay across the bed. His father yanked his shirt up high. Ezekiel trembled and listened. The belt buckle whacked him across his buttocks before he'd readied himself. He clamped his hands over his mouth, but a muffled cry escaped. The leather found the soft spot behind his knees. His body bounced on the bed as the strap hit his back.

At last, his father stopped. "Folly is bound up in the heart of a child, but the rod of discipline drives it far from him."

He daren't move as he listened to his father's words.

He hated his father, but respected him, too. He should not have read the comic, but the devil had tempted him, and now he paid the price. His head throbbed, and his ears felt like balloons. He heard his three cousins scuttle down the stairs as his father left the room. He didn't blame them. His father's idea of discipline was a horrible experience.

He heard his father call the cousins. "Get your backsides up here." The stairs clattered as the boys ran to obey.

Ezekiel stuffed his handkerchief into his mouth to stifle the sobs. He wanted to cry, but that would warrant another thrashing. He'd received more punishment than any child he knew, except for his cousins. Why was his father so mean to them?

He huddled in the corner, and the air turned icy. A deep voice filled the room.

"Son, you are chosen. Endure this chastisement, my son, and I will strengthen you. I have great plans for you. Be not afraid, for I am with you, always."

He froze, and his eyes widened. He looked up and saw a mysterious cloud vanishing above his wardrobe. An audible voice. It must be God.

He'd been told about this phenomenon, and he'd read it in the Bible. Samuel had been about his age when God chose him, and called him three times. And now, he'd been chosen. He pressed his hands against his chest, fingers splayed. Me! He wants me!

He wanted to run downstairs and tell everyone, but remembered his father's leather belt. No, he'd keep this miraculous event secret. They didn't deserve to share it.

His heart raced. The chosen one, what did it mean? It didn't matter. It was good, and he was special.

As Ezekiel bowed before the desk in his prayer closet, Azazel appeared behind him. The dark entity lowered his chin and looked down and sneered. How he loved this assignment.

Gressil, his minion, appeared at his side, his eyes glowing a faint red. Together they'd watched the boy grow into the man before them. They were gratified with their mission. The nine-year-old boy had been shaped and molded into the self-righteous, bigoted soul that knelt at the desk.

Azazel turned to Gressil. "What next?"

"I think the woman's son, don't you?"

"As you wish."

Azazel's body darkened and pulsated with energy. He leaned closer, his voice barely audible. "Welcome, my son. You've served me well, but there is more to do."

Ezekiel bowed lower. "Just tell me your wishes, Lord, and I will faithfully serve you," he whispered.

"The woman is strong. Even her child's death hasn't broken her. The son must pay the price for his mother's sins."

"Thy will be done, Father."

The entities watched Ezekiel struggled to stand. The man had grown infirm, and soon it would be time for a new assignment. They faded from view, but didn't leave.

Ezekiel's body creaked, and he grabbed his chair for balance. Arthritis plagued him more and more every year. His mind raced as he blew out the candles. The boy, what was his name? Yes, Alistair. Wasn't he at Cambridge University? It could be tricky, making it look like an accident.

He locked the door behind him and made his way down the stairs and dialed his two most trusted disciples, Archie Redford and Eamon Tierney. They arranged to meet at the house later.

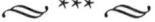

Archie and Eamon arrived at the rectory together, and Millicent showed them into the drawing room where Ezekiel sat before a log fire. He motioned them over, opened the meeting with prayer, and settled back to talk.

"The Lord has spoken to me, and he wants to punish Xantara further for her sinful ways," he said, smiling slightly. "The Lord told me we must punish her through her son."

Archie looked pleased. "What's the plan?"

"He's in Cambridge, at university. I want you both to find an opportunity to kill him. By accident, of course."

They plotted through the night, until they were satisfied with their fool-proof plan.

In Cambridge, Alistair reclined on his bed, controller in hand as he battled "The Assassins" on his Xbox. He knew he played it more often than he should, but it relieved the pressure of pursuing a double degree in modern history and economics. At last his avatar fell under the swords, and he decided to get some sleep.

The school had assigned him a small room. It held a bed and desk, but the main attraction was its privacy. He was in his second year, and loved the independence from his mom and dad. His sister's death had devastated him, and he couldn't bear to witness the anguish on his parents' faces.

He brushed his teeth, then checked his schedule. Great. Tomorrow's lecture wasn't until early afternoon. He settled down and programmed his mind to dream about girls.

The next day, Archie and Eamon drove to Cambridge in Archie's old station wagon. Archie, a careful driver, took several hours to get there. The famous spires appeared, silhouetted against the skyline, and they looked for a cheap bed and breakfast.

A terraced house with a B & B sign promised a warm bed, and they were soon settled in a plain room. A nightstand separated the twin beds covered with flowery bedspreads, faded but clean. The reasonable tariff included a breakfast of bacon and eggs.

After their hearty English breakfast, the pair set out to find a gas station. They filled up and asked directions to a hardware store.

It didn't take them long to find the tool they wanted, a fine-toothed hacksaw. The checkout clerk bagged it, and in minutes they parked near Alistair's entrance. They sat under an elm tree that shaded the narrow road opposite the dorm next to a green space signed "The Park," which consisted of a small grassy courtyard with several oak trees. A pleasant spot.

Archie looked at this watch, then across the road. He nudged Eamon. "That's him." They watched Alistair exit the dorm and walk down the road toward the campus.

"Come on, let's do it," Archie said. They crossed the street to the apartment block and went through the vestibule into the student car park.

"There, that's his car." Archie pointed to Alistair's Ford Mondeo, which had seen better days. Rust had eaten its way along its seams. As they approached it, Archie glanced about him. They were dressed in the dark-blue overalls they wore for farm work, so anyone seeing them would think they were mechanics called in to fix the car. Archie slid under it and found the brake cables.

"Saw."

Eamon took the hacksaw from its bag and passed it to him, and Archie frayed both front brake pipes. Ten minutes later, he slipped back out. The car was old, and even a mechanic would think the pipes burst with use. Satisfied, they walked back through the vestibule into the street, grinning at each other as they headed home.

The political lecture centered on the government's response to the global financial crises, and Alistair took notes. Yes, he suffered from the poor economy, that's why he drove a crock of a car!

He hadn't heard from his mother for over a week now, and he was worried. When he arrived home, he phoned his father.

"How are you, and how's Mom?"

"Not too bad. Work's busy, so I haven't had much time to think."

"And Mom?"

"She—she's away in Cornwall. A friend asked her to stay a while."

"I'll drive down for the weekend, keep you company," Alistair said.

"No, don't do that, son, I'm fine. Keep up your studies and concentrate on work. Exams are important, and I want you to do well."

Alistair replaced the receiver and shook his head. He could accept that his mother wanted to get away, but his father's odd attitude mystified him. His stilted voice didn't sound right. Alistair decided to drive down to Wiltshire, anyway.

Saturday morning he threw a few items into his backpack, picked up his laptop, and went to his car. He hoped the engine would catch. He turned the key and smiled as it sprang into life.

As he backed out, he relaxed. Yes, he needed a change of scenery himself. A country weekend would revitalize his batteries, and it would be good to see Dad.

He drove through the cobbled streets near his university. He appreciated the history and how fortunate he had been to secure a seat in his chosen college. He relaxed and whistled a tune. It was a bright day, ideal for a drive.

Alistair pulled onto the main road and pressed the accelerator down. The car responded well, for such an old model. The beautiful day warmed his heart as he watched the bright yellow rape fields flash by. He accelerated faster and raced down the open highway.

A white figure appeared, right in front of him. He hit the brakes hard. No pressure! He pumped the pedal but it went straight to the floor, useless. His heart pounded in his chest.

No brakes…

Chapter Sixteen

The boy huddled under the covers behind the closed closet door in Brooklyn, New York. He should be asleep, but he loved playing games on his sister's Ipad, and he needed more tokens to reach the top level of Smurf Village.

He hoped his parents wouldn't notice the faint glow under the closet door. He could picture his mother now, wagging her finger. "An eight-year-old should be in bed at eight." She would be furious if she found him awake after midnight. He fought to keep his eyes open to complete the level, maybe another fifteen minutes.

He heard a scream, and jumped. Another scream. It sounded like his mother, or his teenage sister. He held his breath.

"Leave them alone!"

It was his father's voice.

He crept out and looked around the bedroom door, over the bannister. Light spilt out into the hallway below, and he saw his mother's feet lashed to a chair in the living room. A strange man held a gun to her head.

He sneaked back into the closet and pulled a duvet over him. Footsteps pounded up the stairs and he heard his bedroom door open, and the light snap on. He pressed his elbows tight against his body and hunched over. The closet door opened, then shut. He heard the bedroom door slam, and let out a long sigh.

What was going on?

Jeremiah glared toward the husband as he waved the gun between the wife and daughter, duct-taped to chairs. "Look at them. Do you want me to shoot?"

He read fear in their eyes, and inwardly smiled. He used his odd appearance to intimidate, and once again, it worked. His face, hair, and body were snow white, his eyes colorless. He favored black. The contrast of his dark clothing caused a strong reaction in most people. His accomplice stepped forward and held a sharp boning knife against the man's throat. He pressed hard enough to release a thin trickle of blood that ran down the husband's neck.

The bank manager's face blanched. "Okay, I'll help you. Leave them alone, I'll do what you want."

The third man returned from upstairs. "All clear," he said.

Jeremiah checked the women's tape, and apparently was satisfied. "Let's go in his car."

The two men bundled the bank manger into the back seat and drove off, and Jeremiah followed. They drove to the Wells Fargo Bank, five blocks away, and into the staff parking lot behind the building.

They needed this money. The Phineas Priesthood was out of funds.

~ *** ~

The boy listened. The house was silent. What should he do? He couldn't leave the closet to get a phone, but—but wait! He could send an email. The message wasn't so easy, but he tried. The Ipad belonged to his sister, and he accessed her email account.

He typed, Man at the house. Has gun. Help, please.

About to press "send," he stopped and added his name and street address. He pressed the mailbox button to send to everyone and hoped he'd be believed.

107

The teen heard her laptop ping. An email.

She put her geography book down and viewed the message. At first she discounted it as a prank, but realized the late hour. Her friend's little brother should be asleep. She hesitated, then picked up her cell phone and dialed 911. "I've received an email message from a friend. There's a gunman at their house."

She could hear the operator tut. "Is this a hoax?"

"Her dad manages Wells Fargo Bank."

Thank goodness, the operator folded. She promised to send a patrol car to both house and bank.

***

Hours later, Jeremiah and his men found themselves in custody, facing felony charges for aggravated robbery. The court arraignment was scheduled for the next day, with little chance of bail.

They appeared before the judge, who set bail at one million dollars each. Jeremiah smiled. It wasn't a problem.

As soon as allowed, he called his cousin Ezekiel and explained the situation. "One million dollars, how soon can you pay it?"

Ezekiel laughed. "I'll have you out in a couple days."

The guard took Jeremiah back to a holding cell. A large black man with frizzy grey hair occupied one of the two bunks. Jeremiah sat as far away from him as possible. What were the guards thinking, putting him in with a filthy black man? Ezekiel had better hurry up with the bond.

***

Two days later, when the authorities let Jeremiah out, they confiscated his passport. His first job was to replace it. He went to his apartment and called up favors, and within hours a new European passport was delivered to his door.

He then called a friend he'd made at an export company. "I need to leave the country. Can you help?" Within hours money exchanged hands, and he was soon aboard a container ship heading for London.

Days later, Ezekiel drove off in his Jaguar XJ to collect his cousin. He drove through the Port of London dockyard, parked, and watched the container ship dock. His cousin appeared atop the gangplank dressed as a sailor. Authorities checked his papers, and allowed him to leave the port. He descended the gangplank and Ezekiel threw his arms around him. It had been years since Jeremiah moved to the US, and he couldn't wait to catch up with his news. As they drove along the M4 toward Wiltshire, Ezekiel realized how much he looked forward to his cousin's company. They shared a special camaraderie, were of like minds.

Jeremiah followed Ezekiel into the church and down to the crypt. Ezekiel gestured toward the woman.

"Here she is. Xantara Pembroke, witch extraordinaire."

Jeremiah glanced into her cell and drew in a sharp breath. "She could be my twin! Is she...?"

Ezekiel banged the bars. "Yes, she's Albino. Strange isn't it?"

Jeremiah moved closer, and the woman stared back. "But her eyes...they're beautiful. It's not possible."

"It's the devil's magic." Ezekiel backed away, and glanced about. "Sorry, but you'll have to hole up here for a while. I'm sure the FBI's already on your tail. But first I want to know what you've been doing."

They went back upstairs to dine. Ezekiel opened a bottle of St Claire Pinot Gris, from a boutique vineyard in New Zealand, his favorite. Both men sat on a pew with a picnic basket between them. Jeremiah's mouth watered as Ezekiel pulled out chicken, smoked salmon, salad with crusty rolls, and a block of Tasmanian Brie. Jeremiah enjoyed his food and dug in with gusto. The wine tasted superb. He lifted his feet onto the front bench and relaxed.

"Now tell me something about your life since I saw you last," Ezekiel said. "Did you take that architect job the New York people offered you?"

"Yes. I went directly from getting my degree in London to the wilds of Manhattan. They offered me a generous package and promised I could use my own designs. It was too good to turn down."

Ezekiel wiped his mouth with a linen napkin. "And how did you keep your soul safe, among all those heathens?"

Jeremiah smiled, thinking. "It is different there. White power, a bunch of gun-crazy air-heads. The mainstream churches are downright useless, what with women preachers, advocates for gays, that sort of thing. I looked around for a church with similar ideas to your father's. "

"And did you join any?"

"Yes, I met Jack. He led a small group called the Phineas Priesthood, one of many scattered through the States. His group only had five members, and they invited me to join them."

Ezekiel poured more wine and finished the bottle off. "I've never heard of the group before. What do they believe in?"

"They believe God chose them for this priesthood from the deeds of Phineas, son of Aaron. I'm sure you know the story."

Ezekiel indeed knew it. Phineas was the guy who killed an Israelite man caught sleeping with a Midianite woman, and God sent a plague because of the immorality. This pleased the Lord and he granted Phineas an everlasting priesthood.

"It's in Numbers. Numbers twenty-five, I think," Ezekiel said.

"Right. You know your Bible, cousin, inside and out."

Jeremiah crossed his legs, and smiled. "We fund the priesthood through—well, ingenious ways. This time they caught me. The police said a little kid emailed his sister's friends, who alerted them."

"Ingenious ways? Scams and robberies, I'm sure. So, where's Jack now?"

Jeremiah smiled. "You know me, Ezekiel. I don't like to follow orders. I groomed the other members over time, then organized the perfect job."

"Go on."

Jeremiah leaned back, studying his hands. He looked up. "I was architect of a new building for an export company," he said. "I of course knew all the building's intricacies and that made it easy for the group to—well, to relieve them of excess funds."

"What happened?"

"I set a trap for Jack. The safe held the Christmas payroll, and he wanted it. I gave him the map and the safe's combination, but I mixed the code numbers. He set off the alarm, and—well, he's inside for fifteen years."

Ezekiel grinned, then became serious. "You haven't changed, but remember the four of us are equal. Do I make myself clear?"

"We're family."

Ezekiel relaxed again. "What're your plans?"

"Big ones. With your help, of course, and that of Malachi and Obadiah. I want to set up Phineas Priesthood pockets throughout the UK and Ireland."

Ezekiel packed the basket and wiped out the wine glasses. "I'll ask Malachi and his two sons over for a few days, and your brother's nearby in Swindon. We have a second exorcism planned for the witch, and maybe a little extra entertainment to celebrate your return."

"Sounds good. Sounds very good."

CHAPTER SEVENTEEN

The underground room grew claustrophobic and the candle sputtered out. Xantara focused on a single ray of moonlight filtering through the air brick. A full moon, the time of healings at Avebury Circle. And she couldn't be there.

There'd be no healing ceremony performed tonight, unless they asked her mother to complete the quorum. Her mind, sluggish from sleep, conjured up pictures of Imogene. Perhaps she would sense her daughter's presence, and encourage her to appear. She turned on her side. It made no difference. Her back, made sore by the barbed jacket she was wearing, was uncomfortable in any position. If she could reach the stones, the Light Beings would heal her in an instant,.

Xantara's mind drifted to past ceremonies. She saw strange figures of light flitting among the stones on Avebury Circle's perimeter, then come closer until they passed through the sick patient. The Energy Guardians didn't know for sure who or what they were, but without question, they were essential for an effective healing.

The scene played out before her of a young boy diagnosed with leukemia. Jamie Cameron lived in an outlying village with his parents and three older siblings. The doctors had told the distraught parents there was little hope for his recovery. Xantara had heard about his plight from her husband, after his once-a-month meeting with local doctors at a pseudo-Irish Swindon bar, where they swapped stories for mutual support.

The Camerons readily agreed to keep the rites secret. Hope in any form, however tenuous, was welcome. They arrived at Avebury circle around eleven, when the full moon was at its height. The Guardians had arrived an hour earlier to prepare for the main ceremony. The fragrant scent of herbs filled the air as they mixed them with oil to mark symbols on each stone.

As his parents stayed outside the circle, Xantara led five-year-old Jamie toward the center. She smiled down at him, and he smiled back. "This way, little one. We have magic to heal you." The women sang to the drumbeat, calling on the ancients to have compassion for the child, to restore him to health.

The Light Beings, shaped like men but without features, emerged from the Portal Stones and floated toward them. As they glowed and drifted, glimpses of multi-colored auras pulsed around their outlines. They drew closer to Jamie, then, one by one, passed through his body. Their auras glowed, then dimmed, as they appeared behind him. Moonlight bathed the scene as the light forms faded and the Guardians stood watching in silence.

Jamie's face glowed with joy as he ran to his parents. They hugged, and his father hoisted him onto his shoulders.

Xantara trusted the parents to keep their secret. Medical professionals would say it was remission, and not raise their hopes. She loved the healings. The Guardians also benefited, their own well-being strengthened by the other-worldly creatures. Their auras touched them as well as their patients with life-giving power.

A soft glow brought Xantara back to full consciousness. A large entity pulsed and formed into a Light Being, and then another, smaller, appeared beside her. Multi-colored auras surrounded them.

Mesmerized, she watched the larger Light Being approach her, then pass through her body, exactly as she had witnessed at Avebury. The warm flow infused her with strength. Her back pain disappeared, and the hooks felt smooth. She was healed, and the cruel garment somehow neutralized.

She smiled her thanks. Hope returned. She felt at peace, loved, and cared for. The figure of light re-joined the smaller figure.

They communicated with her telepathically. Zazriel explained that Imogene stood beside him, safely in his care. All would be well. She was to trust, and not worry. Moments later the forms dwindled into specks of light which blinked, then vanished.

Xantara's heart filled with joy. Her daughter's second visitation lifted her burden of grief, like a black cloud moving away to reveal bright sunshine.

The Light Beings cared for her. It was as much as she could ask for, even though she longed to embrace Imogene in a physical sense. Now she could look forward to joining her one day, their souls roaming the Universe together.

Jeremiah again followed Ezekiel down to the crypt. He looked around. Yes, he was right. It was the perfect hideout from the New York authorities.

Ezekiel pointed to the cell. "I had my people prepare your room."

Jeremiah noted the warm bedding, food basket, a lantern, small radio and two books. He turned and shook his cousin's hand. "Thank you. It'll do for a while, but don't leave me to rot down here for long."

Ezekiel waved in Xantara's direction. "Your temporary roommate. I'll be down later. Don't interfere with the woman, she's my assignment."

Full after the meal, Jeremiah lay back with his hands behind his head. His bed stood in the ideal position to observe the woman.

Several hours passed. He scratched the back of his head. "Xantara, isn't it?" She stared at the floor. He tried again. "I'm Jeremiah."

She slowly lifted her head. "Jeremiah who? And why are you here?"

He crossed his arms. "Jeremiah Yates. Ezekiel's my cousin. I got into trouble and needed to hole up for a while."

The woman fell silent. He sat up, opened the picnic basket, and lifted out fresh fruit and a bottle of soda. He bit into a crisp red apple and let the juice trickle down his chin. Xantara licked her lips.

"Hungry?"

When she didn't answer, he threw a banana into her cell, and watched her snatch it up and pull the skin off. In three bites it was gone.

He paced up and down, then sat back down, realizing he might as well be in jail as stuck down there. He considered the woman, a captive audience. Why weren't her eyes weak and pink, like his?

"So, you're a witch?"

She said nothing, but stared at the floor.

"As for me, I follow the true religion," he said. "The Phineas Priesthood."

Xantara perked up and looked at him. "Tell me more."

Jeremiah puffed his chest out. "Phineas was the grandson of Aaron, renowned for slaying an Israelite man who lay with a Midianite woman. He founded the priesthood, and today members are selected with great care. We don't mingle with non-believers. It's against God's law."

Xantara stretched and turned toward him. "Is it similar to Ezekiel's beliefs?"

He leaned forward, elbows on his knees. "Yes, but we go much further than him. Some call us terrorists, but our beliefs will be validated when God gives us victory over the US government. America, and eventually the world, will be populated by pure white Christians. The idolaters, yellow-skins, blacks and reds, will all be gone."

Xantara walked over and gripped the bars. "So you'd destroy gays, people of color, and religions like paganism?"

"Yes. The movement is widespread in America, and the US government hunts for our members, hence my presence here. We plan to expand. First, Ezekiel will implement God's agenda here. My brother

Obadiah operates in Swindon, and in Dublin another brother, Malachi, will set up his own Priesthood."

"How do you finance all this?"

He grimaced. "Well, that's why I find myself here. We rob banks. I got caught, so now I have to wait it out in this dump."

"Have you ever considered a broader view? Living a life of love and compassion for your fellow man, for example?"

He grunted and clenched his fists. "My uncle raised me on the true path. There is no other way than God's way."

Xantara lowered her voice. "I'm not a witch, but I do belong to an ancient order, established long before Christianity. What would you say to a greater power that healed a Japanese woman, or an Indian Yogi? God wouldn't heal these people if he favored the white-skinned, would he?"

Jeremiah shrugged. "Your pagan gods don't count. There is one God, my God."

"But Jesus wasn't white. He was middle-eastern, in-between, sort of tanned."

He turned his back. "Shut up, witch."

The next day Ezekiel came back, and he and Jeremiah went upstairs to talk. Ezekiel placed two soft kneelers on the pew.

"Might as well be comfortable. Have a seat. What do you know about exorcisms?"

Jeremiah crossed his legs and paused. "Little, I'm afraid. Not part of our operation, but I'd love to see one."

"Well you shall. I can't let the witch live, of course. Not after the deaths. But let's enjoy the process."

"We need to cut her to let the badness out."

"How about salting the wounds?"

116

Jeremiah made the sign of the cross. "Good, and let's draw crosses all over her body with blessed water. The Devil won't be able to withstand it."

"What do you intend to do with her?"

Ezekiel grinned. "What do you usually do with witches?"

"See you tonight, then?"

"Tonight."

Xantara watched her new companion. Darkness enveloped them, and he turned up his lantern, and tried to tune his small radio. He got only a weak signal, and threw it down. Her nerves jangled as he sat tapping his knees.

"Are you expecting someone?" she said.

He paced his chamber. "You'll find out soon enough!"

The door at the head of the stairs clanked opened. Steel studs from Braxton's boots clicked on every step as he made his way down. The rest followed, a pack of hyenas.

Xantara's stomach knotted as she studied each face. At least Braeden wasn't there. Would she ever set eyes on her husband again, or was this the end? Her lip trembled, and she jammed her hands under her armpits. She was the last prisoner. That thought made her desperate to empty her bladder, and sweat formed on her upper lip.

Eamon turned the key and the cell door swung open. She cringed against the back wall, forcing them to drag her out. They unbuckled and removed her shirt, then bent her over the altar face-up, her wrists secured.

As before, the fundos chanted and chastised her. Her mind wandered, immobilized by terror.

She drifted as the hours passed, until the first cut jolted her back into the present. The second formed a cross on her stomach, and she screamed. Slice after slice, crosses appeared on her milky white skin. Her breasts, her stomach—they even sliced her arms and legs. Could anyone endure such agony?

She screamed again, then froze as Ezekiel's wife Millicent approached her with a salt shaker in hand. She salted each wound as she would her Sunday roast, a small, tight smile on her thin, pursed lips. How could such an everyday object inflict such pain? As the exorcism ritual continued, their voices rose and fell as they intoned the words.

Ezekiel painted the Holy water over the crosses, triggering the salt to run further into the wounds. "Be gone, you spirits of Satan. I command you to leave the woman now!"

Xantara stared past him. What was that? A black mist swirled behind Ezekiel's head, and an image formed. She'd never seen such vileness in her life. As the form solidified she saw three horns on its temple. Its expression was shocking and twisted, its mouth opened to reveal razor-sharp teeth. No one else seemed to see it.

Other forms appeared, each one more gruesome than the last. She was terrified that her heart would stop, then half wished it, to end this madness. She stared wide-eyed, unable to look away from the dark, demonic creatures.

When she believed her wildly beating heart would give out, a Light-Being appeared, then several more. Ezekiel and his minions jumped back. They could obviously see the Light-Beings, but not the evil entities.

Millicent raised her hands. "Praise the Lord, Angels, come to help us," she said.

The Light Beings engaged the entities and a battle raged on, until the negative energy dissipated. The Light Beings formed a circle around the altar and, one by one, passed through her body, healing each wound until her skin became pure once more. The dark entities vanished, and the fundos looked like rag dolls without a puppet master.

Braxton pointed. "Look at her. Her skin, it's clear! I can't believe the angels would heal this wicked witch of a woman."

They released her and threw her back into the cell, and huddled together. The Light Beings' appearance had apparently confused them.

Ezekiel stepped back. "I know. God wants to prolong her punishment. He's healed her so we can torment her again!" He snorted loudly and slapped his sides.

CHAPTER EIGHTEEN

Riordan Yates eyed the five rats on the board, their feet wired tightly in place. He grasped one, and its nose twitched as it struggled to get free. He picked up his Swiss army knife with his other hand and carefully picked its eyes out, and flicked them to the floor.

He found the rats' squeals delightful. He'd played with them since early morning. Among the tiny black-seed eyeballs on the floor lay a tail and a couple of ears. As he prepared to slit their gullets, he heard his father outside and flung a sack over them, dusted himself down, and went out the stall door.

Malachi Yates stood there patting the nose of his choice racehorse, a handsome eighteen-hand bay. "Top o' the morning to you, boy," he said.

Riordan joined his father and brother as they walked along the stalls of thoroughbreds. His father stopped again to inspect his prize animal. "Isn't she a beauty? The Hill of Crockafatha races have given us three years of success, lads, and we'll win again this year. He reminds me of Moses, my childhood hack."

Riordan gave the horse an apple. "What was Moses like, Father?"

Malachi rubbed its forehead. "He was smaller, but chestnut with the same white star on his nose. My uncle made my childhood a misery, but that horse saved my sanity."

Riordan's brother Sean stepped closer. "Did you miss your father?"

"Of course, but I loved my brothers and Ezekiel. We stuck together, but were often forced to look out for ourselves. Yes, an unpleasant man."

The three men finished their tour and gave the stable-hands their orders. The dew sparkled in the sunlight across the emerald fields as they walked home for breakfast.

The hundred-year-old low, whitewashed farmhouse sat on several hundred acres five miles south of Dublin. Riordan looked around proudly. The income from their successful stud and racing stables provided the family with an extravagant lifestyle, and he appreciated the freedom it afforded him. He smiled as he pictured the secret passions he indulged in.

He watched his father pour a pitcher of cream over his oats, and thought how alike the three males were. All striking, with typical Irish coloring, clear green eyes, topped with a thatch of jet black hair. Malachi worked them hard, and he'd built a physique to be proud of. Tall and muscular, he used his strength to considerable advantage on their midnight prowls.

He listened to his mother Molly as she clattered about the kitchen, washing dishes. She knew her place.

Malachi licked his spoon. "We go a'huntin' tonight, boys."

Riordan cleared his throat. "Let's wait outside Duffy's Bar in Waterford Street around eleven. Sure to find a drunk or fornicator there."

His father pushed his chair back. "Good plan, son. Off you go now, see you school the horses well."

Riordan stood with Malachi and Sean on a shadowy corner opposite the pub. He heard the bell call for last orders, and ten minutes later unsteady bodies piled out.

"When Irish eyes are smiling," crooned one lone figure as he crossed the road and staggered down a dark lane. They followed a few feet behind and, before the man left the alley, they rushed him. With seasoned practice they grabbed his arms and plastered duct tape across his mouth in one swift motion. Within seconds they bundled him into the Range Rover and drove off. Five miles of narrow lanes later, they reached the stud farm.

The moon rose higher as the clock struck the hour. Riordan and Sean carried the drunkard down into the soundproof cellar and dropped him next to a thick post. Malachi handcuffed the man's wrists around the wooden support and left the tape across his mouth. The drunk slumped forward and passed out. They would work on him tomorrow.

The next day Riordan went to check the sinner. His position hadn't changed, so he gave him a sharp kick. No response. He kicked him harder. "Wake up, you good-for-nothing."

He pushed the man back with his foot and noticed white cheesy stuff oozing out around the silver duct tape. The face, chalk white, gave him pause. Could he be dead? He gagged and covered his nose from the smell of rank bile. Then it dawned on him. The man had suffocated on his own vomit.

He went off to find his father. "The sinner's dead, and we need to dispose of him."

Sean creased his brow. "We can put him in the old silo."

Riordan nodded. "Good idea. Potassium hydroxide will dissolve the body. No problem, Pa."

Malachi smiled. "Good solution. Well done, lads."

Riordan stood all day at the stone kitchen bench, mixing the chemicals. He'd banished his mother from the room, but not before she'd fetched him her largest preserve pans. He measured and mixed for several hours to produce enough concentrate capable of liquefying an entire human body.

Long after the stable lads slept, Riordan and his brother transported the pans of corrosive powder in one wheelbarrow, and the body in another, over the rough fields toward the silo. They reached a horse trough at the field's edge, and struggled to carry it to the silo entrance. Riordan stiffened as a gunshot echoed into the night. It sounded close. He motioned to Sean to stand in front of the wheelbarrow.

A young stable-lad walked out from behind the silo, shotgun in hand, a pair of rabbits slung around his neck. He looked disconcerted as Riordan confronted him. "No harm, sir, a couple of rabbits for the stew pot, that's all," he said.

Riordan stepped forward and eyed them. "Two beauties. Well done."

The familiar rage rose into his chest. He grabbed the rabbits and twisted the wire around the boy's neck. It made an effective garrote. The gun dropped to the ground as the lad's body crumpled.

He turned to his brother. "Let's get a move on." Between them, they pulled the trough into the silo base and dropped the two bodies into it. "Fetch the stuff."

Sean lifted the heavy pans from the wheelbarrow and removed their lids. They each took a handle and tipped the pan over the trough's edge, partially emptied it, then moved it toward the head. They repeated the process with the second pan, but this time they moved it toward the feet. They scattered a thick layer of hay over the mixture and grinned.

Riordan turned to Sean. "The old silo hasn't been used for years, but we have to make sure it remains undisturbed. We'd better block the entrance."

Sean nodded and helped him replace the wooden door. They wheeled the barrows back to the machinery barn, which lay away from the main stables and sleeping quarters. No one could hear Riordan fire up a one-man, walk-behind forklift and guide it out of the barn. He directed it toward the silo, using it to pick up a large boulder on the way to block the entrance. Satisfied, he and Sean returned the machine and went back to the house.

His father stepped out of the shadows. "How long will the mixture take?" he asked.

"A couple of days, and all traces of them will be gone. It leaves a brownish liquid behind."

Malachi and Sean went off to bed, leaving Riordan to carry the preserve pans around the back. As he primed the pump to wash them out he thought about his father's horse, Moses. What a terrible childhood! Thank God his own father didn't beat him and his brother. He could be stern, but seemed opposed to corporal punishment. For them, anyway.

As he pumped, the terrible rage he'd experienced earlier sprang up again. It had a life of its own. Maybe he'd inherited the sinful genes. The rages increased of late, and arose without cause. He'd looked forward to tonight, and the possibility of a fight. The night had turned out better than expected. The stable-hand's murder released the tension. The dark feeling became harder to control, and the possibility of demon possession plagued him.

Molly passed the phone to Malachi. "It's Ezekiel. Jeremiah's back."

He smiled and took the phone. "Wonderful news! How is he?"

"Good,' Ezekiel said. "I'd like you and the lads to come over. We have a rare ceremony planned which you'll all enjoy."

"Sounds good. Can you meet the ferry?"

"Of course, let me know the time. My nephews are in for a treat."

Malachi replaced the phone and rubbed his chin. What did Ezekiel have in mind?

CHAPTER NINETEEN

Detective McCullage sat at his desk, puzzling over the kidnap victims. He stroked his chin and looked out the window. A knock at the door startled him.

"Come in."

A tall, thin man strode into the room and stuck out his hand. "Simon Barley, County Surveyor. I'd like to have a chat."

"Sure, have a seat."

"It's about the girl crushed by rocks, on The Isle of Angels." He paused. "I don't think it was an accident."

"Why?"

"Well, I inspected those buildings a week before it happened, and they were in good condition. No way could they have collapsed without help."

McCullage frowned. "Why wait until now to tell me?"

"I've been on holiday, at our time-share in Marbella. I didn't hear about it until we got back this morning, and I came straight here."

"Do you have a copy of your report?"

"Right here." Simon removed papers from his briefcase and handed them to him.

McCullage scanned the document. Clearly, the inspection showed the lower chamber and tower safe. He stood and held out his hand. "Thank you, sir. Mind if I keep this?"

"It's a copy, all yours. I hope you find out what happened."

McCullage saw the surveyor out and sat back in his chair. Yet another anomaly. Each day brought another surprise.

That afternoon, McCullage scrambled over the rocks and skirted what now seemed to be a crime scene. Behind the ruins he noticed crushed brambles and rocky debris. It looked as if someone had recently stepped through the stones, then scaled the building. He bent over and peered at the ground. Damn, no clear footprints.

He climbed higher, and saw fresh marks on the stones. They could be scrapes from a crowbar or a chisel. The solid rock crumbled, sending a shower of debris down the wall. No, too risky for him to go farther. He decided to send for an experienced team with the proper equipment.

McCullage walked the ruin's entire perimeter, then followed the island's edge. Often the foliage was dense and interlaced with brambles, and he couldn't get close to shore. A short distance from the tower he came across a sandy cove, and noticed recent drag marks across the sand. A boat. Was it a clue, or a casual fisherman? On closer inspection, he found a partial footprint. He'd get the forensic team out here, then question the parents.

Unable to brake, Alistair twisted the wheel with all his strength. He missed the white figure by inches. He gripped the wheel as the car flew over the ditch and ploughed through a hedge. Leaves and branches flew into the air like a green hurricane. His car careened across the field, destroying crops in its path. Finally it came to rest against a lone sycamore tree, thirty feet into the field.

He gasped for breath as his heart pounded in his chest. Bloody hell! His stiff, white fingers still gripped the wheel. He couldn't let go. The circulation returned to his hands and he uncurled his grip, finger by finger. He dropped his forehead onto the wheel and composed himself.

He opened the door, got out, and walked back to the road. It stretched straight for a mile in each direction, empty. The roadside ditch was full of dirty water. He used a stick to move overgrown branches and searched for a hundred yards, both ways. No body! Perhaps the bright sun had conjured up an imaginary person.

A car sounded in the distance, and he waited. An old farm truck came into view, and he waved the farmer down. The old man lowered the window.

"Need a lift?"

Alistair pointed back toward the large gap in the hedge. "Someone appeared in the road right in front of me, and I swerved. My car's over there."

The farmer stepped out of his truck, and they walked back and climbed through the ruined hedge. The car had cut a swath through the wheat crop.

The farmer scowled. "Why didn't you stop? Going too fast?"

"My brakes failed. I can't understand it. The car was serviced last week."

The farmer inspected the car, as did Alistair. Plainly, it would have to be towed. Even if the brakes worked, the suspension looked damaged.

Alistair touched the roof. A write-off for certain, and no insurance. But thank God, the accident happened on a straight stretch of road. Whatever or whoever the white figure was, it saved his life. A few miles further on and he would have been in heavy traffic.

Alistair's thoughts tumbled as the farm truck rattled along the highway. His mechanic had checked and relined the brakes only a week ago. How could they have failed? He was sure he'd seen a white figure, but maybe it was just reflected sunlight.

The farmer dropped him off at the train station. He sat on a bench, hands stuck in his pockets, as he looked up the track. The train pulled into the platform. He boarded, got off at Cambridge, and caught a bus to the mechanic's garage and explained his problem.

The mechanic looked perplexed. "I replaced the brake linings and checked the whole system," he said. "I'll send a tow truck out. When I find out what happened, I'll call you."

The next day the mechanic called. "Alistair, it's Mick. The brake pipes were cut, almost clean through. Did you upset somebody?"

Alistair stood silently, thinking. His friends would never do such a thing, and he couldn't think of a single person who would. What if he'd been killed? How would his parents handle another death?

Braeden picked up the phone. "Alistair, how are you, son?"

Horrified, he listened to Alistair's account of the accident. "Thank God you're all right! Look son, don't worry. I've needed a four-wheel drive for the countryside, and you can have the Renault. Why don't I come up to Cambridge Saturday and we'll go car-shopping together?"

"Sounds great, Dad. Thank you."

"See you Saturday. Love you."

Goosebumps popped up all over Braeden's skin. He couldn't bear to lose his one remaining child. He shivered. It could so easily have happened.

The nurse popped her head around the door. "A detective McCullage to see you, doctor."

"Thank you, show him in."

He didn't recognize the man when he walked in, and he'd met plenty of police officers at the hospital. "Please sit down. How can I help?"

The detective cheeks flushed. "I'm so sorry for your loss, but I need to ask you a few questions."

Braeden's mind raced. Did he suspect Xantara's absence? After all, the hairdresser and grocer disappeared.

"Thank you. Please ask me anything."

McCullage pulled at his collar. "Has anyone a reason to harm your daughter? Or you, through her?"

Braeden stiffened. "No, no one. Why?"

"The county surveyor certified the tower and surrounds safe a week before the accident. I'm sorry, but I have to investigate her death. It may not be an accident."

Braeden's eyes widened. "My son's newly lined brakes just failed. He could have died. Could there be a connection?"

The detective leaned forward and frowned. "Tell me what happened."

Braeden pressed his lips together. What should he do? He decided to relate his son's misadventure. He had no choice.

"I'd like to speak with your wife," the detective said.

Braeden tried to smile, but wavered. "Xantara's away. She's with a friend in Cornwall, but I expect her back soon. A couple days, at most."

"Okay. As soon as she's home, have her call me." He handed Braeden his card.

As the door closed behind the detective, Braeden's fist flew to his mouth as if to stifle a scream. The headache returned, and tears formed in his eyes.

He laughed. The edge of madness seemed a mere heartbeat away!

McCullage frowned as he drove back to town. Two people missing and a strange death, all in one small village. Something was wrong. And several people had disappeared and reappeared in Swindon. That was weird, too. Were they connected?

He returned to his office, despite the late hour. He wrote details of all the unexplained events on post-it notes, stuck them on his white board, and studied each one. He touched the pen to his lips, then wrote another note and stuck it in the center. The doctor's wife. He didn't know why, but his gut told him all roads led back to her, the mother of a possibly murdered child.

He hoped she would be back soon.

CHAPTER TWENTY

Braeden drove fast. Until Ezekiel's accusations he hadn't given Xantara's Avebury activities a thought, but today he would discover the truth. Yes, he'd been too self-absorbed for his own good. The New Age stuff had seemed harmless, and opportunities to ask about it had passed by.

Until now.

He parked his new Land Rover in front of Avebury Manor and briefly admired its facade. Recently, the owners had turned the grand house into successful tearooms. He strode in and headed toward the former library, now a delightful room with cleverly sited tables adorned with the best Wedgewood china. The book-lined walls gave the room character akin to the nineteen thirties, and the old books' musty smell mingled with freshly brewed coffee.

He spotted Bryony near the window. She looked up and smiled. "I've ordered us tea and cakes." A teapot, kept warm with a knitted cozy, sat on the table next to a double-tiered cake stand filled with dainty selections.

She frowned. "Are you all right? Have you heard from Xantara?"

He sat, straightened his tan slacks' creases, and neatened his navy jersey. "She's fine. I expect her back in a couple of days. Bryony, I want to support her when she comes home, but I know little about her friends and interests. Would help me understand?"

"What can I tell you?"

"Look, I know you and her other friends are involved with New Age stuff, but she and I have never discussed it. Now, I'm curious. I want to understand her, to know how she feels now that Imogene's gone."

"Yes, I'm sure Xantara wouldn't mind my telling you. She always said you'd scoff because of your scientific mind."

Braeden felt like an idiot. Of course she'd been reluctant to confide in him. He crossed his arms. "So, is witchcraft involved?"

Bryony laughed. "That's crazy. We're Guardians of Avebury circle, heirs of ancestors who have protected the circle for almost five thousand years. The Bible first mentioned witches two thousand years later. Our power's real, not invoked with spells or magic, but given to us freely by the Star people. With their help, we heal the sick. Haven't you noticed your patients often don't return?"

"Come to think of it, yes. So genuine healings do happen? But recently, the clinic's been overflowing. Do you know why?"

"That's because Xantara's gone. We need her to complete the energy path."

He eyed her. All this was new to him. Was she serious? "So, what do you believe? Do you have faith in God, or an afterlife?"

"Yes, God is the divine designer, and made multiple universes. He sends the Star Beings to help us. You and I consist of pure energy, and our spirits continue in another dimension after our earthly death. At times they reincarnate and occupy another body."

Braeden paused, his teacup in mid-air. "Then Imogene's spirit exists, and she may even return in a new body."

"Find comfort in truth. All's love and only love. The Spirit's purpose is to help us support and love one another. Life needs nothing else."

"How can you be so sure it's the truth?"

"Our order's history has shown us many times," she said. "Thousands of villagers have received healing over the centuries. With Spirit's help, we perform miracles every year."

He placed his cup down and looked past her. This was quite the opposite of Ezekiel's perspective. What's truth? What's Spirit? Obviously, the dark evil witchcraft stuff lived in Ezekiel's imagination. After the lawyer's actions, why should he accept a word he says?

Bryony waved her hand in front of his face, and he refocused. "We'll never know the whole truth while we occupy these bodies," she said. "Spirit reveals the truth when we pass over. Imogene knows the reality now, and one day, when you join her, so will you."

A waitress came over, and he ordered a second pot of tea. The room had emptied, but it was still half an hour until the café closed, and he wanted to hear more.

Bryony shifted in her chair and frowned at him. "I have to tell you our Guardianship's in trouble. The healings have all but ended."

"Why?"

"Well, if the eldest daughter of each of the eight original Avebury village families isn't present, we can't generate the critical mass of energy. Because of Xantara's absence we've cancelled the next healing ceremony. We did try with Sabina, but it didn't work."

Braeden closed his eyes to think. He'd taken the Hippocratic Oath promising to heal and sustain life, and to do no harm. Surprisingly, their philosophy fit right in with the values he treasured. His head spun. This last week his whole world had been shaken, turned upside down, then shaken again. He couldn't make sense of the chaotic thoughts racing through his mind.

He stared hard at Bryony. "So The Guardians end with Imogene's death? No more healings?"

"Yes," she said.

"But over five thousand years other young women must have died without birthing a successor."

"No, but under-age women have been in line, which meant waiting until they reached eighteen. The Light Beings healed all their illnesses and injuries to ensure continuity."

"Incredible! Over five millennia. Who are the Light Beings?"

"Energy light forms. We think they come from the Sirius star system. They appear near the portal stones, then pass through the patients with their restorative power."

Braeden stroked his chin. "Come to think of it, I can't remember Xantara being ill. Not even a cold or the flu."

"You must realize, we receive healings for the smallest ailments," Bryony said. "Our immune systems are made healthy, and our cells renewed, at each ceremony." She laughed. "Haven't you noticed Xantara and her friends look young for their age?"

"Now that you mention it…"

She stood. "We'd better leave. The waitress wants to close up."

Braeden hugged her and smiled. "Thank you. Now I understand."

Bryony sighed and nodded. "You're welcome. If I can help, please call."

Braeden drove slowly back to Monkton St Michael. Perhaps he would never learn the truth about life, but Xantara and her friends seemed closer to God's message than Ezekiel's lies. It was time to face the truth.

Braeden headed toward the rectory. On impulse, he turned toward the hill. Perhaps the crypt door was unlocked. As he grasped the entrance door handle and inched it open, he heard voices.

"What did you do with the body?" Eamon asked.

Fremont Braxton laughed. "No problem, he's sausage now. I chopped him up and mixed him in with off-cuts of beef and pork."

An icy chill ran through Braeden. So, Jonathan was dead. Now he was complicit in a murder. His fears for Xantara grew. This madness had to stop, and soon.

Ezekiel's powerful voice echoed around the nave. "Our mission failed. Xantara's other child still lives. We'll move her to the island tonight, and deal with the doctor. He must never know what happened to his daughter."

Braeden slunk away, stunned. He returned to his house and sprawled over his sofa, a glass in hand, staring at the half empty whisky bottle.

Images of his crushed little girl flashed through his thoughts like a horror flick. He roared with pain. They'd killed his precious daughter, tried to kill Alistair—and now he and Xantara were in their sights.

What should he do? He couldn't trust himself anymore. He was an educated man, yet they'd sucked him into their irrational beliefs. He swapped the glass for the bottle and drained it.

Eventually he made up his mind. What did it matter if the medical panel struck him off, or authorities sent him to prison? He couldn't let them continue this vendetta against 'sinners.' He had to save Xantara.

Despite the pounding alcohol-induced headache, he would visit the manse. Pastor Mark Benedict would know what to do. He was confident he didn't know about or condone the fundo's beliefs.

An alcoholic stupor came over him. He would rest, just for a moment. Almost immediately he sank into a deep sleep.

CHAPTER TWENTY-ONE

She heard them coming.

The fanatics trooped into the crypt, much as jury members filed back into court to deliver their verdict. Guilty! It was plainly written on their faces.

Where was Braeden? Fear rose inside her. What would happen without his moderating influence? Four men she didn't recognize accompanied Jeremiah. Who were they?

As they gathered around her cell a key grated, and Freemont Braxton entered the chamber. She bowed her head and clutched her stomach. Her heart thudded against her ribs, fear-based arrhythmia.

The butcher grabbed her arm and pushed her through the door. She fell onto a rough flagstone and grazed her knee, rubbed it, and moaned. Sadist, he relished that. What was happening? Where're they taking her?

The others stepped back, and Braxton pulled her up and shoved her ahead. Millicent pushed aside a hanging church banner depicting Christ as the Lamb of God, to reveal a hidden passageway. Ezekiel stepped into the blackness, lantern held high.

Xantara's patients often mentioned tunnels rumored to crisscross between the village and the church. Several believed they linked the church to the island tower, under the lake. Could they be taking her there? For what?

Xantara staggered along, her heart pounding. Her claustrophobia set off a panic attack. It was a dreadful dream, a nightmare! The walls closed in, the darkness smothered her. She heard only the scrape of feet and the elder's heavy breath. The air smelled dank, mixed with sweat from her clammy hands. She sporadically touched the walls to avert a fall.

She stumbled along for ages. At last a faint light appeared, and grew brighter as she neared the tunnel's exit. She emerged and looked up. The tower, looming above, illuminated by a full harvest moon. She was inside the ruin's base.

Xantara looked around, and saw no avenue of escape. What would they do to her? Frightful images flashed before her eyes. Would they stab her? Drown her? What? She clapped a hand over her mouth. The fear of death flowed through her bones and a scream formed, but she held it in. Her backbone strengthened. She wouldn't give them the satisfaction.

They dragged her into the courtyard, and she stared in horror. A stout wooden pole stood dead center. At its base lay bundles of twigs and brush, arranged like the spokes of a Catherine wheel. She shuddered. It was a terrible fate, beyond even her imagination.

A primal scream sounded, and her heart felt about to burst. She clutched at her throat and fell in a dead faint. Blessed oblivion closed in, a welcome void.

She came to, with the sounds of an incantation, her hands chained behind her. Smoke tendrils filled the air. She could smell them.

The Fundos surrounded her, their faces manic. "Burn, witch, burn."

Ezekiel waved his fist. "Wicked woman, go to hell. Burn forever, in the fires of Sheol."

They marched, circling the fire like a pack of hungry wolves. With each rotation they chanted louder, their venomous words echoing around the courtyard.

The pungent smell of wood burning overwhelmed her nose. Her eyes watered. Wildly, she looked around. Curls of pale, silvery smoke rose as strange, misty phantoms that twirled in the light of kerosene lamps.

It must be a dream. No, a nightmare, of gargantuan proportions. As the smoky clouds and the heat increased, the ring of flames moved toward her like a giant mouth threatening to engulf her. She drew a breath and gasped as acrid smoke burnt her throat. A shriek of terror echoed across the island, so piercing it almost reached the village.

Her eyes watered profusely as the hot gases engulfed her. Coughing, spluttering, she panicked. She tried to breathe. No oxygen! As she choked, a strange peace overcame her. She relaxed and welcomed gracious oblivion.

The pain vanished as she soared high above the island. She looked down at the crowd, swirling and dipping like dervishes, and laughed. How ridiculous they looked. Dark demonic faces lit by flames hovered above, urging them on.

Xantara felt exhilarated. A tunnel opened before her and she sped down it. Faster and faster she flew. So, this was death. An incredible intelligent light beckoned her onwards. She let go, and a delightful sense of freedom moved her forward. The light sparkled. Rainbow-colored rays pirouetted around her. How beautiful!

Expelled into a wondrous world, she marveled. Below, fields of iridescent green glowed. The sky was so blue and clear, it hurt her eyes. She blinked and cleared her vision. Brilliant flowers of every hue caught her breath. Waterfalls, rivers, streams, sparkled as they meandered through the exotic landscape.

The scene filled her soul with wonder. She flew on.

"Welcome, my child."

The soft voice pierced her reverie. She turned to the light form flying beside her. He guided her down, toward a colonnade of Doric columns.

"Come." He led her inside the Grecian building. A vaulted ceiling crowned the open room. An ornate carved structure, resembling a Vatican font she'd once seen, dominated the center.

The Light Being picked up a stone goblet, filled it from the font, and offered it to her. She drank. Life-giving energy coursed through her, and she found her voice.

"Am I in Paradise?"

"Not exactly. Heaven isn't a simple place, it has many dimensions."

He turned his head toward a doorway across the vast chamber, and she followed his gaze.

"Mommy, mommy!"

Her daughter stepped through the door, raced across the room, and flung herself into her arms. Xantara's heart surged with joyous electricity, a jolt of sheer pleasure. She hugged her and showered her with kisses.

She sobbed with relief. "Baby, my baby." They both laughed and cried, until the Light Being intervened.

"For now she must stay, and you must return."

"No! I want to stay with my daughter. I have nothing back there."

He gently coaxed the girl away, pointing at the doorway. Imogene walked toward it, looking back over her shoulder. Mother and child locked eyes, until the moment she stepped out of sight.

"Please, don't separate us."

"Have faith, you'll see her again. Soon." He moved close and whispered a message in her ear. Her eyes widened, and she smiled.

A sudden rush of air surprised her, and the tunnel flashed past as it sucked her backwards.

Chapter Twenty-Two

"**D**ad, wake up!"

Braeden opened one eye. "Alistair?"

His son glanced at the empty whisky bottle, and stopped shaking him. "I'll brew coffee." He walked toward the kitchen.

As Braeden sat up, a premonition of disaster rushed through him. "Never mind that. We have to save your mother."

Alistair turned to him. "What do you mean?"

"Grab the car keys, you drive."

"Where to?"

"Pastor Benedict's house. I'll fill you in on the way."

Braeden told Alistair the whole story as they sped through the village to the rectory. They parked and hurried up the path, and he banged the knocker. A television blared inside, then was silent.

Mark Benedict opened the door, and frowned. "Braeden, Alistair. What brings you here so late?"

They pushed past him. Inside, Braeden glanced into the living room, startling the pastor's wife, who sat on the couch. He turned back as Mark walked in.

"Pastor, you have to help us. They're going to kill Xantara."

The pastor froze. "What do you mean? Who's going to kill Xantara?"

Braeden told him the story. His shoulders collapsed as he hung his head. Mark closed his mouth and compressed his hands.

"That sounds preposterous. Ezekiel's hard-edged in his faith, but this? I can't believe it!"

Braeden looked up, his cheeks burning. "It's true, Pastor, every word. What should I do?"

"You say he's been using the church?"

"Yes, that's where they kidnapped Xantara."

The Pastor rubbed his chin. "He has no right. I asked him to leave the church months ago. His views upset the congregation. He accused long serving members of outrageous deeds, and the council voted to excommunicate him."

"The group meets at his house, but he often uses the church."

He looked hard at Braeden. "I'm sorry, but I have to call the police."

Mark called, and they waited in silence. Soon the door knocker sounded, and detective McCullage and two officers entered. They sat, and Braeden told his story once more.

McCullage tapped his knees. "You say they intend to kill your wife tonight?"

"Yes."

"Well, what're we waiting for? Pastor, bring the church keys."

The men piled into cars and raced toward the church. Mark opened the main entry, then the crypt door. They rattled down the stone steps, constables in front lighting the way.

Empty.

McCullage inspected the cells, then turned to Braeden. "Any ideas?"

"They mentioned the island. Maybe they took her there."

They exited the church and looked across the lake, where a faint light appeared near the tower. McCullage phoned for reinforcements, asking everyone to meet at the quay.

Within minutes the police launch docked, and they climbed aboard and roared off toward the island. The spray stung Braeden's eyes as he stood in the prow, waiting to jump ashore. They throttled back and approached the island quietly, cutting the engine as soon as they docked. As they neared the ruins, loud voices drowned out any sound of their approach.

From behind rocks and bushes, they saw the bonfire's flames lick the stake. With horror, Braeden saw a figure among the scrolls of smoke. Alistair roared and sprinted over, the police following. He ignored the chanters and furiously kicked away the brush and logs, clearing a space around the pole.

Braeden watched, paralyzed. Alistair untied his mother and lifted her to safety. She didn't move. Too late! She was dead, and he was responsible.

"Dad! Dad, come here."

He walked listlessly toward the remnants of his family.

"You have to try, Dad."

Braeden felt for a pulse. None. For his son's sake, he would give her CPR. He tilted her head back and lifted her chin to open the airway, pinched her nose, and clamped his mouth over hers. Two breaths. He pushed his hands against her chest. Thirty pumps, two breaths. Thirty pumps, two breaths.

"Dad, she's moving. She's alive!"

Braeden's eyes filled with tears. He cradled her in his arms and sobbed.

With the police focused on Xantara, Braxton and Ezekiel quickly led the faction into the hidden tunnel. They stumbled along, guided by a solitary light ahead. The cousins and nephews went ahead, consigning their followers to darkness as they disappeared around the bend.

Braxton shouted after them to wait. No response. He stopped as the light faded altogether, and the others collided with him. The darkness was so oppressive and profound, he felt buried alive. The butcher roared. "Bastards, how dare you leave us?"

The tunnel lit up as light forms appeared. The human shapes weaved around them. Millicent called out. "Angels, we're saved!"

Freemont Braxton grinned. God was on their side. He noticed other forms appear behind the Angel Beings. Demonic forms. Who were they?

Lightning flashed, the ground shook, and debris fell on his head as thunder echoed down the tunnel. Fear etched on the women's faces sent an icy chill down his spine. The tunnel collapsed, and darkness fell.

Braxton's soul regained consciousness, and he recognized he existed in Spirit. The light forms had vanished, and the demonic figures closed in. He watched each soul appear, one by one, as it released its physical form. The group of souls looked dazed as the demonic forms surrounded them.

More Dark Entities gathered. Braxton watched the demons tug and pull the women, their souls screaming in absolute terror as the demons dragged them away. A pit of fire opened below them. Their final, fiery destination.

A fiend turned toward Braxton. "Not me!" he shrieked. You're wrong! I'm special. I belong with the angels."

A three-horned face grinned inches from his own face. "You're right. You're so special." Talons sprang from the demon's fingers and hooked into his soul. The pain became unimaginable as they dragged him into the flaming pit.

McCullage and the police fanned out to search, but the perpetrators had vanished into the night. He left two officers behind and returned to the boat. He would deal with them later, but for now Mrs. Pembroke needed the hospital. He allowed Braeden to carry his wife aboard the launch, and they sat together.

As they headed to shore, a spectacular electrical storm lit up the sky. Light flashed around the island, lighting up the whole area. He turned to watch as each lightning bolt transformed the tower into a diamond scepter. He'd never seen anything like the storm's brilliance. Lights danced and darted among the trees and ruins.

A loud crack cut through air. Everyone turned toward the fortifications. Forked lightning struck the tower, the impact so powerful the turret shook violently, dislodging rocks. The tower crumbled before his eyes. With awe, he realized what a close call they'd had. Anyone in the courtyard would have been crushed under the avalanche.

Braeden carried his wife ashore into the care of the paramedics. Sirens blared as the ambulance left. Alistair threw his arm around his shoulder.

"Don't worry, Dad. At least Mom's alive. Pastor Benedict has offered me a bed for the night, and I'll be at the hospital first thing. Rest, sleep if you can."

They handcuffed Braeden and drove him to Swindon Constabulary. He lay on a molded concrete bed which felt like bedrock, under a hard florescent light. Thank God she was alive.

But what would become of them all now? When would he see Xantara again?

Would she want to see him?

CHAPTER TWENTY-THREE

McCullage rubbed his eyes and tried to focus on the incident board. After the late night, he'd only managed four hours sleep. What was the next step? He'd question Xantara Pembroke later, but first he'd ask the magistrate to have her daughter's body exhumed.

His door opened and his boss, Inspector Burroughs, entered. He studied the post-it notes and cleared his throat.

"I see Mrs. Pembroke's center-stage. Are you any closer to tying things up?"

McCullage straightened. "Yes, sir. Members of a religious sect are doing it. Can you believe it?

"Christians?"

"Well, at least they once were. They've been kicked out of the church. Pastor Benedict gave me a list of names, and it seems a lawyer from Monkton St Michael is the ringleader. Ezekiel Yates.

"I've heard the name. Are they in custody?"

"No. Their cars were still parked at the church last night, and I found a tunnel entrance in the crypt. I followed it as far as I could, but found it blocked. The pastor believes it's linked the church and island."

"And?"

Like always, the Inspector was acting like a bulldog.

"We can't find them. We visited their houses, and they're gone."

The inspector leaned against the table's edge. "What's the next step?"

McCullage shrugged. "I'll know more after I talk with Xantara Pembroke. I'm also trying to get her daughter's body exhumed."

The inspector nodded, frowning. "You've already talked with her husband, I assume."

"I'll interview him first. He's a victim as well as his wife, and has been through a lot. Losing his daughter may have unhinged him a little."

"Well, keep on top of it."

The inspector left, and McCullage downed the dregs of his coffee, picked up his case, and walked across the quadrant to the holding cells. The guard doffed his cap.

"Morning, sir."

"Morning, Charles. I'd like to interview Pembroke, please."

The guard left to get him, and McCullage sat at the small table. The room, bare, cold, with murky green walls and metal furniture, wasn't conducive to encouraging inmates to open up. The guard returned with Braeden, who stared at McCullage with a shocked expression. He didn't look like the doctor he'd visited at the clinic. He'd aged twenty years, his face ashen and sunken. He hung his head as he sat across the table.

The detective relaxed. "How are you today?"

The doctor didn't answer. McCullage extracted a voice recorder from his pocket and switched it on.

"I'd like to hear your account again. From the top, please."

Braeden opened his mouth to speak but his voice croaked, and he stopped. "May I have some water?"

McCullage poured some from a pitcher on the table, and Braeden sipped it. He set the glass down and told the detective what had happened from the moment his daughter died. He paused and looked up for the first time.

"Please, may I visit my wife?"

McCullage returned the notebook to his jacket pocket. "I'll address that in a moment. But first I have to tell you your daughter's body is to be exhumed. I'm sorry for that, Braeden, but apparently she was murdered.

You're free to leave, but there may be future charges brought against you."

Tears welled up in Braeden's eyes. "Thank you. Thank you so much,"

"Can I give you a lift? I have to interview your wife first, but then you can see her."

The detective left Xantara's hospital room, and she nervously waited for Braeden. Alistair had just brought her a change of clothes, and was waiting for her in the car. As she was taking the overnight bag into the small bathroom to change, Braeden appeared beside her. She jumped.

Braeden kissed her cheek. "Are you all right? I'm so sorry. Please forgive me."

She turned away. "I don't want to talk in this place. Please wait until we get home."

She changed and soon they walked down the concrete steps to the car park in silence. Alistair jumped out and climbed into the back, and Braeden settled behind the wheel and engaged drive. As they neared the village, she squeezed his knee.

They arrived home, and Xantara walked straight into the kitchen and filled the kettle.

"Sit down, honey, let's talk."

Alistair went toward the back door. "I'll be in the garden if you need me."

Braeden sat at the table, his back straight and stiff. She placed a mug of fresh coffee before him and sat opposite, cradling her mug.

"I do understand, love," she said, smiling. "I know more than anyone what you've been through. What we've both been through."

"You don't hate me?"

"Haven't I told you for years that love is everything? Without it, the entire world has zilch." She paused. "Don't you see? One mistake doesn't wipe out a marriage, a lifetime of love."

Braeden reached across the table and held her hand. "You could have died."

"But I didn't! You saved me. You came through when it mattered."

She stood and moved behind him, gently slid her arms around him, and kissed the top of his head. He groaned, and she pulled him up from the chair and encircled her arms around his waist and laid her head against his chest. They stood there for a long time, until she heard the back door open. Alistair had returned from the garden.

"Hi, Mom, Dad." He breezed in, checked the kettle, and made himself a cup of coffee. He came to the table, and they all sat. Xantara clasped his and her husband's hands and looked from one to the other.

"I have something to tell you," she said. "I had a near death experience."

She looked quickly at Braeden, expecting an air of skepticism to cross his face. It didn't. She was pleased to see they both listened with interest as she related her experience. When she reached the part where Imogene hugged her, her voice cracked.

Braeden squeezed her hand. "I wish I could have held her."

Her voice steady, she looked straight at him. "Well, you will. And soon."

He pulled back. "Don't torment me, please, just when I am coming to my senses. What do you mean?"

"The Light Being promised she'll be brought back to life in two days, at the Summer solstice."

"That's not possible! How on earth can he promise that?"

"Look, you both know the circle's amazing healing powers. We've healed many people before. He promised we can bring her back."

Tears welled in Braeden's eyes. "My love, she's dead. The circle's power can only be used to heal. Well, live people, I mean."

"Before I was drawn back into my body, the Light Being told me what to do."

Braeden shook his head violently. "But how can they resurrect her? She's been buried for over a week. They're exhuming her body this afternoon."

"Why are they exhuming her? What's going to happen?"

"They think that she was murdered, and they want to perform an autopsy. She will be held in the morgue until it has been arranged."

"Perfect! That will give us the opportunity to retrieve her body. We can break into the morgue before they do the autopsy."

Braeden stared at her. "Her body...it will have deteriorated. What if your experience was simply a lucid dream?"

Xantara pressed her lips together and stood. "It wasn't a dream. Could you live with yourself if we didn't try? We have to do this."

The three planned their next move.

CHAPTER TWENTY-FOUR

Ezekiel, his three cousins, and two nephews stumbled about in the tunnel, choked by clouds of dust. They had escaped the rock fall by a whisper. He looked back. The rest of the team must have been buried. He thought fleetingly about Millicent. He would miss her after all their years, especially her splendid meals. But, no time for sentiments now. He had to get to safety.

They emerged into the crypt, then made their way outside and ran down the hill. "We can't use the cars, or the police will know we're not dead," he told the rest. "We'll have to walk."

They took shortcuts across the fields, and as dawn broke they reached the former government underground city's Beachwood shaft entrance. Exhausted, they trudged the last mile to the compound proper. Obadiah led them to a dormitory, and they collapsed on the military bunks.

Obadiah clicked off the lights. "They won't find us here, so relax and get some sleep. We can plan our next step tomorrow."

Ezekiel awoke and found the washhouse, which had six showers and a row of latrines. He welcomed the hot shower as he washed the grime and dust off. He opened a locker, found a military camouflage jumpsuit, and struggled into it. At least it was clean.

He saw a map of the facility printed on a tin plate screwed to the wall, found the chapel, and made his way there. A simple brass cross stood on a rosewood altar, a matching brass rail in front. He sank onto the royal blue kneeler, bowed his head, and put his hands together.

"What went wrong, Lord? But at least we killed the woman before they arrived."

"Son, you have done well, but the witch lives," a voice said.

A heavy feeling settled in his stomach. "Xantara's alive? How did she survive the fire?"

"Her husband and son revived her."

He gripped the brass rail tightly, until his knuckles turned white. "I'll get that horrible woman, if it's the last action I take on this Earth."

He returned to the others. They found the kitchen, and sat around the table. Obadiah formed a steeple with his fingertips. "We have enough supplies to last us for years," he said.

Ezekiel told them of God's revelation. "We have to find a way to get rid of her for good."

Obadiah smiled. "The summer solstice is due in a few days, and thousands of New-Agers and other weirdoes will gather at Stonehenge. Last year over thirty thousand attended the festival. She's sure to be there."

Ezekiel's stomach fluttered, and his heart pounded. "You're right, the witch will be there. Just think—we can rid the world of a multitude of sinners in one glorious act. I like it! I like it a lot. But how?"

Obadiah motioned for the group to follow him. He turned left, then right, then right again, emerging into a steel-lined corridor. He stopped at a solid door, clearly marked: 'Armory, Permitted Personnel Only.'

He pulled the key from his pocket, opened the door, and stood back. A collective gasp escaped from their mouths as they viewed the contents. There, on row upon row of grey metal shelves, were explosives, guns, knives, other weapons and munitions of every kind. Jeremiah moved closer. Chemicals, detonators—why, this was a terrorist's dream!

Obadiah grinned and puffed out his chest. "And I know how to use it all."

Malachi chose a repeating rifle, and slung it over his shoulder. Jeremiah picked up a large commando knife and a small handgun. He turned to Obadiah. "Why's this stuff still here?"

Obadiah winked. "Remember, I was responsible for decommission. I simply told them I'd cleared it out." He re-locked the door and motioned them to follow him back to the kitchen.

Ezekiel joked as they cooked a meal, which consisted of reconstituted packets of meat and vegetables. He sniffed the plate, then tasted it. It wasn't great, but they were hungry enough to overlook the bland taste.

They cleared the table, and Obadiah spread out an ordinance map of Stonehenge and its surroundings. He pointed out a hideout, only half a mile from the stones. "Ideal. I'll build the explosives with electrical charges, and detonate them from a distance." He pulled out a prepaid cell phone. "This'll do the trick."

"You have only two days until the equinox," Ezekiel said. "Can you do it?"

"No problem. There are even manuals for this stuff, but I won't need them."

Ezekiel kept Obadiah company as he spent hours at the kitchen table building the deadly devices. He made twelve, and at Ezekiel's suggestion packed them with ball bearings to maximize the damage.

They were ready.

Jeremiah used his reconnaissance experience, gained by scouting banks and businesses to raise funds for the Priesthood. He knew what to do. He dressed in black, then smeared khaki green and dark greasepaint on his face to blend with the terrain.

Obadiah led him through the tunnels to a secret exit, where an old army issue motorbike he'd used before leant against the wall. Together they pushed it outside and mounted it. Time was short. They rode across the darkened fields to Stonehenge, twenty miles away, not daring to use the headlights. The Salisbury Plain was exactly that, flat and featureless, ideal for an off-roader.

A dark shape grew larger as they drew near. Obadiah stashed the bike in nearby bushes and they descended into a Celtic Barrow, a Neolithic burial plot. Several small chambers led off the central one. Obadiah stashed the explosives and lit a lamp. "This is a long barrow," he said. "Mind the bones."

Jeremiah paced up and down. "Let's get on with it."

They laid out their sleeping bags, then finished arming the explosives. Jeremiah trekked across the fields toward the prehistoric monument, stark against the skyline. The crescent moon gave little light, but enough to let him use his service-issue night goggles. He grinned as he imagined the hordes of souls that would assemble here the next night.

He crouched just outside the circle, cut a foot-wide square of grass, dug a hole in the revealed dirt, then planted a device and carefully replaced the sod. Gradually he made his way around the monument, digging, planting, and covering up. Soon the twelve deadly devices were set.

It had taken him nearly two hours to set all the explosives. As he patted the last piece of sod in place a security patrol swept by in a Land Rover, its roof-mounted searchlight sweeping the circle. He hid behind a rock and waited silently until it went away, then made his way back praying for victory over the enemy, the unsaved.

He struggled to find the Barrow entrance, until Obadiah flashed his torch briefly to show him the way. "All done, and no problems." He clapped his brother's back, and yawned. "Time to sleep. We'll need all our energy at dawn tomorrow." He pulled bracken over the entrance, making it almost invisible.

An hour before dawn on the twenty-first of June, Jeremiah checked the crowd from a distance. Thousands jostled for prime position in and near the circle. He crouched down and licked his lips, his heart pounding. They are all so unsuspecting!

One hour to go.

CHAPTER TWENTY-FIVE

Helen's last client flounced out the door, and she closed it with a groan. It had been a difficult reading, and her armchair beckoned. She sat, and as she watched the embers glow she pondered over the week's events. Sybil's dire fate seemed clear, and even her own readings predicted disaster.

The phone rang. "Sybil, how are you?

"I'm good. What time should we pick you up in the morning?"

"Better make it four. That's early, but you know how crowded it gets. I hope I get some sleep tonight."

"What's the problem?"

Helen stretched. "I'm plagued by nightmares. Terrible disasters, blood, bodies, you name it. Spirit is trying to give me a message, and the dreams won't stop until I get it. Even the Tarot foretells catastrophe, and soon."

"How terrible! Is there any chance of a mistake?"

"I don't think so. The troubling thing is, I don't know yet exactly what the dreams foretell, and when it will happen. I'll go to bed now and see if I can get clarification. See you tomorrow."

Helen poked the fire and damped the embers. Tomorrow was a big day. She loved the summer solstice ceremony at Stonehenge. They went every year, and she looked forward to the outing.

As she changed into her nightdress she felt a familiar flutter in her tummy. Her gut warned her to be wary. Maybe they should sit farther away from the monument this year.

155

She lay in bed, eyes wide open. Almost every Tarot card this week predicted death, destruction and injury. She'd watered-down the truth to protect her clients. The Tarot's message was vague, difficult to pin down. What was she missing?

Helen rolled onto her side, and asked her Spirit Guide to enlighten her through a dream. She tossed and turned for a long time before falling asleep. The dream came again. Indistinct pictures flew past, loud bangs and screams sounded, and dead people piled high. The recent Boston bombings in America had upset her. Maybe that was it! The incident must have played on her mind, affected the cards, and produced the nightmares. Poor souls, what's the world coming to?

Bryony checked her patient's temperature—still high—and updated his chart. She glanced at her watch, then at the darkness outside.

It was time.

She tiptoed down the ward, dappled by light from an occasional lamp, checking her other patients. They were all quiet, except for the occasional insomniac still reading. She stepped into the security office.

"Hi, George. How's life?"

He stretched his arms above his head. "Quiet. And this damned arthritis is a literal pain in the backside."

"I brought a cup of hot chocolate. How's the match?" She motioned toward the small black-and-white television showing a replay.

He clicked the mute button and turned to her. "The team's useless, and I could do with company."

Together, they half-heartedly watched Chelsea play The Wanderers, like a silent oldie. As she and George chatted, she made sure her body hid the surveillance monitors from him.

Braeden swiped his card through the reader and poked his head around the hospital back door. He held it as Xantara and his son slipped past him. Alistair held his nose as the morgue odor hit them. "What's the rotten, sweet smell?" he whispered.

Braeden moved toward the desk. "Decaying bodies. The antiseptic never covers it all." He picked up the body register and scanned the list. Imogene Pembroke, locked drawer TN657. He rummaged around the desk drawer and found the pass key.

Xantara touched his arm. "Look at this inscription. 'Life is eternal, and love is immortal, and death is only a horizon; and a horizon is nothing save the limit of our sight.' It's written by Rossiter Worthington Raymond. So true, don't you think?"

Braeden released the trolley brakes and pushed through the freezer doors. Inside, a bank of bright, cold, steel drawers covered the opposite wall. He found drawer TN657 in the second row, and jacked the trolley up until its base was level with it. "Xantara, keep watch," he whispered.

He unlocked the box and eased the tray out onto the trolley, lowered it, and pulled the sheet back. She looked just like an angel. She'd been buried for over a week, but there was no sign of decomposition. Bryony had told him Guardians didn't age much. Well, they must decay at a slower rate, too.

Steps echoed down the corridor, and the trio froze. Braeden pushed the freezer door shut silently and switched off the light. The steps disappeared into the distance. Braeden was sure his heart rate had doubled.

"We'd better get a move on."

Alistair picked up his sister's body. His six-foot frame carried her with ease. Braeden shut the door and replaced the trolley.

Six minutes left to get out.

As George watched television, fully engrossed in watching Chelsea win, Bryony rewound the security tape back half an hour. Anyone who checked the footage later would find nothing amiss. She checked the watch pinned to her bodice and jumped up.

"Well, break over, better get back. Have a good one, George."

Done. She almost skipped along the corridor. They'd be away now, thank God. And she would leave soon for the dawn ceremony.

Braeden's family approached the car, which he'd parked in a dark spot where there were no cameras, and he clicked the door-locking remote. He helped Alistair lay Imogene across the back seat, climbed into the driver's seat, and looked over his shoulder.

My precious girl, I hope and pray you can live again.

He engaged the gears and headed toward Avebury, making sure he stayed within the speed limit so he wouldn't attract police attention. As he drove, he mulled over his interview with Detective McCullage.

"I've told you everything I know," he recalled saying. "Please believe me. I had no idea of their true intentions, none."

McCullage stared at him. "Doctor, you've been through a lot, and it unhinged you for a time. I've children of my own and can't imagine how I would react in similar circumstances. But you're not free of guilt. I could charge you with minor infractions, but I won't. You've cooperated, have no prior convictions, and have a good standing in the community. But I expect your full support to settle the matter."

Relief flooded through Braeden. "Thank you. Thank you from the bottom of my heart."

The detective gave him a warm double handshake, compassion in his eyes. "Doctor, you're free to go."

~ *** ~

Helen's friends knocked on her door just before dawn. She offered them hot punch, to support the long vigil. They filled the car with blankets, picnic baskets, and tea flasks.

A long traffic column crept toward Stonehenge. Already thousands had gathered, but they managed to squeeze their car into a small space on the grass verge. They found it muddy underfoot as they trekked nearer the monument. From experience they'd donned their trusty Wellington boots. The crowd packed into the stone circle. Dante's Inferno came to mind, except this multitude wore clothes.

They stopped half a field's length from Stonehenge, near enough to experience the excitement and anticipation. They found a bare patch and laid out their blankets, and settled down to wait. She heard a pan piper as he moved among the throng of alternative life-stylers, his haunting melody adding ambience. In the distance, a juggler tossed his clubs into the air above the crowd.

Helen soaked up the atmosphere. "Isn't this exciting, girls?" She loved to watch people, and it helped to pass the time. All shapes and sizes walked by. Families with young children mixed with older couples, and many Bohemian types in quest of new experiences. Women passed in elegant robes, flowers entwined in their hair. Two carried small cylindrical drums, tapping in rhythm as they sauntered about. Helen recognized them as Earth Goddess worshippers.

The Druids were evident in their distinctive coarse linen ceremonial dresses, and she pointed them out to a first-time visitor sitting nearby. "Many people believe the stones exist to worship the Earth Goddess," she said. "Look—there's the heel stone. The rising sun casts a shadow right through the middle, and the phallic symbol impregnates the Earth Goddess stone. See those two stones? They represent the cervix and the uterus. My sister came here because she couldn't conceive, and now she mothers five. She believes the stone's power cured her infertility."

Helen reminisced over her first solstice experience as a young woman of the Flower Power generation. They thought they could change the world. She'd worn a multi-colored miniskirt and a flower in her hair. Her mind jumped to the pimply faced boy who drove her there on his scooter. Whatever happened to him?

In the mix of disparate humanity were UFO believers and other alternative thinkers. Some believed Stonehenge guided alien spaceships. She imagined that over four thousand years the stone circle represented many beliefs, now lost in antiquity.

She could see her friends were engrossed in their own memories. She shifted her position, and wished she had brought a picnic chair. Age, God's cruel joke. Sybil offered her a chicken sandwich, and she realized she was very hungry. Yes, time for breakfast.

 ***

A red stag jumped over Braeden's bonnet, bringing him out of his reverie. An omen? He shook his head. Now he was crazy. Could Imogene live again? He couldn't get his head around the idea. It seemed impossible, inconceivable.

As they neared Avebury circle, Xantara asked him to stop. He pulled into a lay-by and waited while she changed into a simple white robe and donned her Silver Star necklace. As they neared the stones she guided him off-road and through the grass, until they neared the Portal stones.

Well, this was it. The smallest chance was worth the risk.

He lifted Imogene from his son's arms and they made their way through the growing crowd toward the ceremony site. His daughter felt cold, but her soft body molded into his arms. Her face, chalk white, matched the Guardians' white robes.

Misty cold air hung about the shadows as the Guardians lit candles and placed them in niches around the healing stones, and silvery jingles filled the air as they shook small tambourines. The occasion's sacredness rooted Braeden in a quiet stillness, an atmosphere alive with pregnant expectancy.

His wife had explained the ceremony was a celebration of life and fertility, but first the energy must build. His skin tingled as the vibrations expanded alongside the musical rhythm and chanting. The atmosphere became electric, and they reached the critical mass. The Light Beings appeared near the Portal stones.

Could they restore life to their child?

Xantara sang and the other women joined in, their melodious murmurings sinking and rising. He found the sound comforting. They motioned for him to lay Imogene on the altar stone, and he did so with reverence and stepped back. The pallor of her face worried him, the effort seemed impossible. My faith is weak. Perhaps I'd better stand outside the circle. The chant grew louder and faster, as the guardians held hands and circled the child. As they swayed, he felt the energy reaching a crescendo.

Braeden watched the Light Beings pass through Imogene again and again, but saw no response. He couldn't believe he was witnessing this. It went against all his beliefs and training. The incredible forms were like wisps of smoke, but he could make out their human shape, even facial features. Who or what were they? The radiant forms glowed brighter as they continued to treat her, but he couldn't overcome his disappointment that it wasn't working.

The Guardians sustained their chant. Their voices rose in a cacophony of sound that sent shivers down Braeden's spine. Their magical crescendo added to the sacred atmosphere. The phosphorescent Light Beings shimmered as they streamed through Imogene's body. They dragged out his anguish. They'd failed, and he wanted them to stop.

The Guardians continued chanting, the melody rising and falling like gentle waves on a quiet ocean. The Portal Stones glowed, and more iridescent Light Beings materialized from behind them. They moved toward Imogene and passed through her body, one by one.

Braeden stared hard for any flicker of movement, any sign of life. No, it can't be! A pink blush kissed her cheeks.

His heart soared as her small chest rose and fell. Her eyelids fluttered, and her lips parted. She opened her eyes and smiled. The Light Beings pulled back and disappeared behind the Portal stones.

Braeden ran to her and scooped her into his arms. Xantara and Alistair joined them. His chest tightened and his pulse raced, as his arms encompassed his reunited family. How would they explain this miracle?

A massive explosion ripped through the crowd, and a blast of air pushed Helen onto her back. The sky lit up like fireworks, and her ears rang. She struggled to her feet, shaken and dazed. She shook her head to clear it and discovered she couldn't hear too well. She looked toward the circle. Bodies lay in piles two or three high.

The dream!

She stood and moved toward the monument. A woman held a small child, her mouth open in shock, as the child's nose dripped blood. She stumbled further into the main camp, tripped, looked down, and recoiled. An unattached leg lay there. This must be the misfortune she'd forecast. Her terrible dream was now a reality.

The closer she got to Stonehenge, the worse the bloodbath. Can those be bullet wounds? The moon shone on silver bits, scattered over the ground. Ball-bearings! That's it, not bullets, but an identical effect. She reached the central mass of bodies. The people near the monument appeared dead. Hundreds, if not thousands, shot to pieces. Arms, legs, even a headless body, made her retch as she stood shocked at the senseless carnage.

She leant against a massive stone for support. It appeared undamaged. Only soft flesh caught the blast's full brunt. The destruction suggested several bombs had exploded. Perhaps it was a terrorist attack, but why? She could think of no group interested in destroying this peaceful ceremony.

Thank God she'd listened to her intuition and chosen a picnic site well out of range. Right decisions can impact and change the future. She sent up a silent prayer of thanks.

Sirens sounded as emergency vehicles snaked along the black ribbon highway across the downs. Helen made her way back to her friends and looked at Sybil.

"Are you all okay?"

"God. Oh, God." Sybil stood, mouth open, looking about.

Helen slipped her arm through Sybil's. "There, there, dear. Come—let's go home."

CHAPTER TWENTY-SIX

What now?

Exhausted, Jim McCullage got out of bed, put his pants on, and went downstairs where Perkins was waiting with the car. Perhaps the constable would tell him more.

He got into the car, and Perkins put it into gear and sped off. "There's been an explosion, sir. People killed and injured."

Jim's adrenalin spiked. "Where?"

"Stonehenge. The Inspector said it could be a terrorist attack."

They reached Stonehenge, and McCullage stepped out of the car and into mayhem. The site boiled with activity, and the whole area was devastated. Lifeless Druids lay dead center, with other bodies splayed out from them piled two or three deep. Glassy eyes stared up as the dawn broke, their corneas glistening in the rising sun. Blood-red patches pooled from several thousand bodies.

The bombers had done their work well. The dead extended twenty yards from the monument into the crowd overflow, and hundreds of injured sat or lay thirty yards out. Paramedics swarmed among them.

The Swindon Chief of Police arrived moments after McCullage. His jacket was unbuttoned, and his cap was jammed on tightly.

"Detective, contact the bomb squad and move the injured further back. No personnel are allowed near the circle until they give the all-clear."

Jim called The Royal Logistics Corps bomb-disposal squad based in Tidworth, an hour away, then scanned the perimeter for evidence. Bodies blanketed the ground, but even so he found ball bearings, and picked up handfuls. Filthy murderers!

He helped the paramedics until the bomb squad turned up, patching, raising limbs, and holding IV's as he followed their instructions. Well versed in CPR, he used his skills several times as they tended the wounded.

The bomb squad appeared, suited up like astronauts, and moved around the massive geometric stones, stark and grey against the golden dawn sky. Carefully, they inspected each hole and determined the device makeup. When they decided no other bombs remained, they gave the all-clear.

The bomb-disposal team leader handed Jim detonator fragments. "Wireless, electrical—the perpetrators have to be close, for the signal to reach."

Twenty policemen from neighboring towns had arrived, and McCullage decided on a half-mile radius area search. Quickly he sketched a plan in his notebook and sent the men out in pairs, radiating out from the center for the best coverage. They found nothing to connect to the blast.

At mid-afternoon Jim sat at his desk, head in his hands. He would never forget the sights he'd witnessed. The Home Office had ordered a dedicated antiterrorist squad from London to take charge. Jim's caseload was full, and he would gladly hand over the investigation.

The Sergeant dumped the morning newspapers on his desk, and their headlines blazed with the massacre. How did they produce and print this already? He picked up the Daily Mail. "Britain's Worst Terrorist Atrocity." The Sun's headline read "Thousands killed at Stonehenge.'" Even he didn't know how many had died yet, but the truth never stopped the newspapers.

The antiterrorist team reached the station at lunchtime. He shook hands with Chief Inspector Grant, the officer in charge, and directed him to the incident room. The man asked him to sit down and stared at him with dark, beady eyes, made darker by the pepper and salt bushy brows overshadowing them. His manner made Jim uncomfortable, as if he were the criminal. Inspector Grant interrogated him for almost two hours, and drilled in on every aspect he could possibly think of, before allowing Jim to leave for lunch. He hoped he wouldn't see the man again.

Jim grabbed a foot-long sub and hot coffee and returned to his office, shut the door, and slumped into his chair. He felt better with food in his stomach, and the caffeine spiked his energy. After a short catnap he went back to work, rereading the medium's kidnapping report, but couldn't concentrate. Severed limbs, missing eyes, and a dead child all crowded his mind for attention.

He paced the station's corridors, passing white-faced colleagues shocked into silence by the devastation. He heard the Home Office team murmuring together, and caught a glimpse of Grant's thick, wiry grey hair as he bobbed about, wielding a stick near the incident board. He made his way back to his office in time to answer the phone.

"Detective McCullage."

"I'm an attendant at the morgue," the voice said. "Detective, we have a missing body."

Jim frowned into the receiver. "Who's body?"

"Imogene Pembroke, the child. We scheduled her autopsy for this afternoon, but she's gone."

"I'll be right over." He grabbed his jacket and hurried out.

Half an hour later he viewed the morgue's security footage. No one had entered the mortuary overnight, and yet the girl's body had disappeared. This case grew weirder every minute.

McCullage drove to Monkton St Michael to speak to Imogene's parents. He tried the door handle. Locked. He read the clinic door message. "Closed until further notice." The interview would have to wait. McCullage slapped his forehead. Of course! The hospital would have contacted the doctor to tend the bomb victims.

He needed to sleep before he collapsed.

~ *** ~

Jeremiah wiped the camouflage paint off his face. The blast had been spectacular. What a rush! He finished his ablutions as Ezekiel called him to lunch. The extended Yates family ate another bland, reconstituted meal in the military-style kitchen.

Ezekiel swallowed a mouthful and picked up his mug. "Well done, lads. The Lord promises us crowns for every good deed done in his name. We'll be mightily blessed for this day's work."

Jeremiah raised an eyebrow. "The whole operation went without a hitch and the explosions were impressive. The ceremony attracted over thirty thousand blasphemers, and in my estimation we killed at least seven thousand and injured scores."

Obadiah nodded crisply. "Yes, I drove by on the motorbike. Blood flowed everywhere, and I heard people scream in pain."

Ezekiel switched on the radio. "Let's listen to the news reports."

The broadcaster sounded shocked. "So far no one has claimed responsibility for the atrocity. Police found the remains of twelve explosive devices, and suspect a terrorist attack. An estimated ten thousand people have been killed or injured."

Jeremiah clicked the radio off. "This is our chance to introduce the Phineas Priesthood to England, by claiming responsibility. Put the fear of God into the whole country."

Malachi looked up. "What are you talking about? What's the Phineas Priesthood?"

"We're at war, a Holy war. The American Priesthood's aim is to create a pure white Christian population. I want to extend the organization across the world, beginning with the United Kingdom."

Malachi picked at his food. "What's God's word say about this?"

"Well, we know God doesn't accept mixed race marriages, abortions, and abnormal sexual practices. Our duty is clear. We must eliminate as many sinners as possible." He forked a piece of food, stared at it critically, and laid it back down. "The World's had its chance. No one will change; so we must exterminate them like the vermin they are. The Stonehenge massacre is a good start."

Obadiah leant back in his chair. "Perhaps we should give the World a chance to change. You know, announce a commandment that they must."

"They won't, but let's do that." He picked up the food again, and stuffed it into his mouth. "And there's something else. God granted this priesthood to us and our seed, our descendants. Our fathers did their duty, but among us four we've only Malachi's two sons to continue the Lord's work. I suggest we abduct attractive young women and impregnate them. Grow our own righteous army."

Jeremiah looked around the table. "Agreed," they all said.

Ezekiel rubbed his nose. "Like our fathers did."

Jeremiah looked up from his plate. "What do you mean, like our fathers?"

"Didn't you know? We each have a different mother. I got curious about why we weren't alike, and realized you and Xantara are both albinos and could be twins. I looked through his papers and discovered your mother's name."

Jeremiah's jaw dropped. "I was told my mother died in childbirth. Who is she?"

"It's Sybil, the twin sister of Sabina, Xantara's mother. You and Xantara Pembroke are cousins."

Chapter Twenty-Seven

Jim McCullage filled his lungs with fresh air. Thank goodness for a good night's sleep. He shut his office door, leaned back in his chair, and opened the first file.

He winced as he read the teenager's medical record. Tattoos had covered almost a third of his body. It must have taken ages for someone to burn them off with a red-hot poker, at least in the boy's view. Poor kid, he didn't deserve to endure such agony. No one did.

He looked at another case file. By comparison, the medium's experience was mild, yet it had frightened her. Both victims had been imprisoned. But where?

He pulled out a map of the local area. The medium's car ride had lasted between twenty and thirty minutes. He judged how many miles that would have been, and drew that radius on a local map. A vast area.

Both victims agreed religion was the reason for their abduction. What was the connection between these incidents and the island?

He mentally replayed Xantara Pembroke's rescue, then reread her statement. Her account cleared up the mystery of the missing village shopkeepers. One confirmed dead, the other perhaps murdered. Xantara told him they'd carried out the whole sequence of events in God's name. Since the perpetrators were buried under tons of debris in a collapsed tunnel, he had to rely on her interpretation.

He sipped his coffee and read on. Mrs. Pembroke had mentioned another man related to Ezekiel Yates, named Jeremiah. His cousin, she said. He searched online for the name Jeremiah Yates, and found a reference in a New York newspaper, but none in the United Kingdom. Could it be him? The article said he'd bungled a bank robbery and disappeared. Even if that was Yates, the puzzle remained unsolved.

McCullage entered the names Mrs. Pembroke gave in her statement into his laptop's browser. All upright community members, unlikely to commit such crimes. But they clearly did.

He shut down his computer and stood. A break would give his subconscious time to decipher the mystery. As he passed the incident room he saw Chief Inspector Grant inside, biting into a club sandwich. The man signaled him, and he went in and sat in the wooden chair across the desk from him.

"Any progress?" Inspector Grant asked.

"Not yet. It appears to be the work of one group, but who? And why? We have no clue."

The inspector finished his sandwich, and looked up. "So—what are you working on?"

McCullage told him about the strange cases. "It has a religious connection for sure," he said. "But I'm not familiar with the location all the victims described."

Inspector Grant looked over McCullage's head, at the incident board. "You say they kept the victims in an underground prison?"

"Yes. They drove them about half an hour out from the center of Swindon, then forced them to climb down a ladder. They walked for at least an hour after that."

"Down a ladder…" The inspector stood, walked to the board, and tapped his cane against a spot on the map. "Look—there's an underground government city here. They built it for officials in case of a nuclear attack, and later abandoned it."

McCullage frowned at the map. The facility was near Corsham. "Never heard of it."

"It's decommissioned now, of course. In fact, I served in the army with the man who used to look after it, Obadiah Yates."

Obadiah Yates? McCullage scraped his chair back and jumped up. "Thank you! You've given me the lead I needed."

He hurried back to his office, his stomach juices churning with excitement. At last, a breakthrough. He phoned the front desk and requested a Special Operations unit to accompany him, then phoned the army headquarters for permission to search the city.

An hour later, a tow-headed corporal turned up with a key and entrance co-ordinates. His fresh face and earnest manner reminded McCullage of a schoolboy, and he felt old as he and the Special Operation officers piled into the armored van. They wore Kevlar jackets and packed firearms.

The corporal directed them up a farm road, toward a copse of trees. They removed the camouflage of branches to reveal a trap door which opened to reveal several steel steps.

Exactly as the medium had described. Bingo!

Ezekiel glanced at the security monitor and switched off the radio. "The police are here! Hurry, we have less than forty minutes to get out of here."

Malachi wrung his hands. "Where shall we go?"

Ezekiel smiled. "I always knew this day would come. Father taught me well. I've salted a fortune away over the years, so money isn't an issue. And I've set up a hideaway for just this reason."

Obadiah's face lit up. "Where is it?"

"Scotland. I haven't been grouse shooting for years. But first, we have to close our operations here. Obadiah, you can see to that. Jeremiah, you go with him."

Jeremiah followed Obadiah into the corridor, and they hurried toward the tunnel's south end. He tapped his shoulder. "You do realize the staff remain a potential risk for us?"

Obadiah slowed. "What do you mean?"

"We can't let them live. They know too much."

Obadiah turned away, but his brother grabbed his shoulder and turned him back to face him. "If you haven't the stomach for it, I have. We've already killed thousands, so this is no time to be squeamish. Lead me there and leave me to it."

Obadiah stopped outside three closed doors, and pointed at one. "That's where we send out scam invoices," he said. "The girl's name is Thelma. The guy in the next room prints for us, and the kid opposite is our computer tech." He turned and walked away.

Jeremiah entered the first room and shut the door. "How are you, Thelma?"

The slight woman with crimped hair didn't look up. "Good, what can I do for you?"

He moved behind her and twisted her head hard. Her neck snapped like that of a chicken for the pot. One down, two to go!

The print operator stood near the stamping machine, which rattled and banged as the plate rose and fell, checking the print quality. Jeremiah kicked him in the groin and pushed his head under the heavy plate as it came down. The result reminded him of road kill. The heavy old machine didn't even pause.

In the next office the young man's fingers blurred as he tapped the keyboard. Jeremiah wrapped an electric cord around his neck and quickly choked him. The nerd didn't even fight back. Pathetic! He opened the computer and extracted the hard drive, then returned to the kitchen.

Ezekiel stood. "They're almost here. Let's go."

Obadiah looked at him, and winced. "There'll be roadblocks. Follow me."

He led the family to the stores, and flung open a cupboard. Military uniforms hung in a row.

Jeremiah picked out a general's uniform, and Ezekiel took it from him. "We'll all wear regular fatigues," he said. "They'll draw less attention, and fit in well with an army vehicle."

"What army vehicle?"

He smiled. "A Land Rover, of course."

Jeremiah changed into fatigues and followed them to an underground garage. It was empty, except for a khaki tarpaulin which covered an oversized vehicle in one dark corner. Obadiah pulled off the cover to reveal a Land Rover painted in camouflage colors.

"It's a fifties model, but it's clocked less than two thousand miles. I think it'll pass muster. Modern ones look similar."

Jeremiah helped him equip the truck with water, food and weapons. He made sure the fuel tank registered full, and filled two extra cans. Time to go.

Jeremiah watched the others climb into the Land Rover. "I'll follow later. There's a matter I must attend to."

Ezekiel frowned. "What?"

"Look. I'll take the motorbike, and join you in Scotland."

Ezekiel shifted the car into gear. "As you please, but don't hang around too long."

Jeremiah headed off down a corridor. This side trip had better be worth the delay!

The armed response unit entered the first rooms and methodically cleared each one. Jim McCullage noticed a wall-mounted map, which showed the prison block close by. "Come on, this way."

Ten minutes later, they found it. The doors were locked, so they checked for occupants through the observation slots. All empty. They moved on.

McCullage walked into the kitchen. "It's exactly as the lad described," he said. "A steel table, and—look, traces of blood down the legs and underneath. This is the room, all right."

Food scraps littered the table next to six half-full cups of cold tea, but the offenders noticeably absent.

They continued to search, and discovered three bodies. McCullage touched each to check for a pulse, and realized they were still warm. He turned to the Special Operations commander.

"Those people need to be stopped. Look—this equipment tells us they had a substantial business operation. How long have they used this city?"

A uniformed man called out. "Look at this sir, a munitions room."

McCullage looked through the open door. Hundreds of silver ball bearings were scattered across the floor. The commander came up behind him. "This investigation is now a matter for the Home Office," he said.

CHAPTER TWENTY-EIGHT

Xantara and Imogene sat up as Bryony entered the guest bedroom, followed by Braeden, carrying a tray of hot chocolate and biscuits. She set it on the dressing table, and Braeden hugged her.

"We can't thank you enough."

She kissed his cheek. "That's what friends are for. Rest now, and we'll talk tomorrow. I'll settle Alistair on the living room sofa."

Braeden recalled seeing the settee, covered with a handmade quilt. Its vibrant starburst pattern matched the hooked felt rugs scattered over the polished timber floor.

Braeden lay on the bed, and Imogene snuggled down between him and her mother. His heart softened as he looked at his beautiful wife and daughter. It was unbelievable, but the resurrection had happened. Here was the proof. He watched them fall asleep, then stared at the ceiling.

His analytical mind tried to make sense of his live child. His Catholic childhood included tales of resurrections, but how could this modern-day miracle be possible? She'd been dead for over two weeks.

They'd covered the topic in medical school. People pronounced dead had come back to life in the morgue. His professor had waffled on about profound comas once.

Braeden recalled Biblical stories of people raised from the dead. Jesus raised Jairus' twelve-year-old daughter, for one, after she'd died a few hours earlier. He also raised Lazarus, after four days. But were there instances of it happening after a longer period of time?

He consulted his iPhone, using his hand to shield the glow from his wife and daughter. At last he found an example. The gospel of Matthew, chapter twenty-seven, read:

"...and the graves were opened, and many bodies of the saints which slept arose. And came out of the graves after his resurrection, and went into the holy city and appeared unto many."

It had happened at Jesus's crucifixion, too. Jesus was seen several times after his death.

Braeden searched the Internet and found current accounts of people who came back to life. He avidly scanned the pages. Most people had experienced near-death events, visited heaven, and returned to tell their story. A recent account happened in South America, when people returned to life after a group of American evangelists commanded them to in the name of Jesus. People still came back to life, even today!

How would he explain this to others? They couldn't hide her forever.

Imogene awoke late the next morning and looked around. She didn't recognize the bedroom, but smiled at her parents, asleep either side of her. Memories flooded her mind. As the beautiful angel woman had said, her spirit had returned to her body. Gently she kissed her mother's cheek, then her father's. They awoke and hugged her. She laughed.

"Please let go, you're squashing me."

Braeden held her hand. "Are you okay, sugar plum?"

Imogene giggled. "Don't worry, I'm back for good."

Her mother held her other hand, and smiled. "I missed you, sweetie, and I love you to the moon and back."

Imogene grinned at her mother. She always said that. She turned to her father. "Dad, I watched you on the island. I didn't realize I'd died. A beautiful woman appeared and we flew together, high and low, such fun. Her name's Rahmiel and she showed me another world."

Her mother half sat up. "Is it the temple where we met?"

"Part of it. Wasn't it fantastic? But later we went to meet the Council of Elders."

"Council?"

"You know the book Alistair gave me about Greece? The building looked like one of the temples, white columns with a roof on top. Inside the open building, the Council of Elders sat around a marble table. The twelve men moved over and made room for me."

"Weren't you frightened?"

"No, Rahmiel stood behind me. I felt safe with her, and the men were kind."

Someone knocked at the door, and Imogene jumped up to answer it. She opened it and Aunt Bryony entered, carrying a tray. "I guessed you three might like breakfast in bed, as it's a special day." She set the tray down and crossed the room. Imogene jumped into her arms and hugged her warmly.

"Aunty Bryony, how are you?"

"Relieved, now that you're back."

He mother moved over to make room for her friend to sit. "Why don't you join us?"

"Thank you." She sat on the bed's edge.

Her mother turned back Imogene. "What did the men wear?"

"Everything was white. Robes, even their hair and beards. A bit like you, Mom. They said I'd come back to you, and asked me to deliver messages."

"What messages?" The others asked, together.

"The Council aren't happy with the people of Earth, but I can't tell you the messages yet. Rahmiel will tell me when to do it."

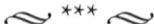

Azazel and his apprentice Gressil crawled into the gloomy cavern. Obscure silhouettes ebbed and flowed as they passed. Hot pools bubbled, discharging clouds of sulfur. Azazel raised his head as they neared their master.

"At your service, master."

Red, malevolent eyes peered from under three twisted horns. His master's foul breath blasted over him. "I have a mission for you."

"Yes, master."

"The child Imogene lives."

"But Ezekiel murdered her, as you directed."

Azazel's master kicked out, and he sprawled across the floor.

"She lives, I tell you! We must destroy her, or she'll ruin my plans. The Council wants her to communicate a message to the World. If she does, we stand to lose many souls."

Azazel gazed at his feet. "But how can we kill her twice?"

"For her death to be permanent we must murder her within the Avebury Circle, at the site of her resurrection."

Azazel considered that for a moment. "I know a human I can use for the job, he's strong and volatile. Consider it done, master."

Azazel hovered over Henry Wall as he sat in his cell. He snorted and punched the wall. Perfect! Azazel enjoyed possession. The physical movement and control were bliss. He slipped into Henry, as easily as donning an overcoat. Henry sneezed and looked dazed.

"Listen, my friend."

Henry yanked his head around. "Go away. You're not real. A random voice in my head."

Azazel used Henry's hand to slap his own face. "Not real? How's that?"

Two prison officers entered the cell, and the older one slipped handcuffs onto Henry's wrists. "Get a move on. Dartmoor prison, for the likes of you."

Azazel sensed Henry wanted to fight. He calmed him down, and the man went quietly to the transport van. The first officer climbed in front, and the second officer, Bert, and his prisoner got in the back. A steel grille separated them from the cab.

Azazel decided to have a little fun. He slipped out of Henry and probed the prison guard's mind. The man wasn't a saint, and an inspection of his recent activities would pass the time.

Bert looked down at his twelve-year-old stepdaughter. Her look of terror excited him. "Stop whimpering. Tell anyone, and I'll do your little sister."

He loved it when Melody cried.

Azazel curled up in ecstasy and probed further.

Bert uploaded his stepdaughter's photos. He relished this sight. Others like him shared their kids' pictures, and he smiled as he uploaded his share. Yes, she was maturing nicely. He glanced over at his family on the couch. His nine-year-old would be a welcome change.

Azazel re-entered Henry Wall. Time to get down to business. He looked out through Henry's eyes. Adrenalin surged through the man's body as he made his move. The chain between the cuffs made the perfect weapon as he swung his arms over the guard's head. Before he could react, Bert's grotesque swollen tongue lay on his chin. Good. The van rattled on, the driver unaware. Henry found the key and unlocked the cuffs.

He banged the grill. "Pull over, driver, your mate's having a heart attack!" The second guard stopped the van, walked around and opened the back door. A hard hit to the head dropped him where he stood. Henry dragged him into the back and locked the doors. He turned the van around and headed back to Salisbury Plain.

CHAPTER TWENTY-NINE

Jeremiah slowed the motorbike as he reached the outskirts of Monkton St Michael. He stashed it behind bushes and walked toward the village. He pulled his cap down tightly and sauntered past the clinic. This must be where she lived. Wait, what does that notice in the window say? "Clinic Closed till Further Notice." Perhaps they're away.

He walked around the terraced block, entered the clinic's long back garden, and checked the windows. All quiet. Good. No one was home. He broke a small window, unlatched it, and climbed in.

The empty rooms looked unlived in, and several days' post lay on the mat. He looked through the family papers for a clue, then found several references to Bryony on the wall calendar. The address book in the desk showed she lived in Avebury. That seems the best bet.

He waited until nightfall, then left. He reached Bryony's house, saw a car outside, and settled down to watch.

As Henry Wall sat outside the hospital in a stolen Volkswagen, Azazel watched the entrance through the man's eyes. At last, Doctor Pembroke appeared and clicked his remote. His car beeped, and he got in.

Azazel kept a car between them as he followed him. The doctor's car stopped outside a house between Sudbury Hill and Avebury circle. Perhaps it was a house call?

Patiently, he waited for the doctor to leave. Finally the door opened, and Pembroke came out with a woman in a nurse's uniform, and they drove off. He could see Xantara and the child through the lighted window. They were alone! He stayed hidden for another twenty minutes to make sure it was all clear, then rapped on the door. Would she answer?

A woman's voice rang out. "Who's there?"

Azazel knocked again. "There's been an accident. I need to use your phone."

The door opened, and Xantara stood in the entrance. Immediately he pushed her inside and pulled the door shut behind them. "Where's the girl?"

She glanced at the stairs. "What girl? I'm alone."

"Don't mess with me. Get Imogene down here right now, or I'll break your neck."

Imogene ran down the stairs. "Don't you hurt my Mommy!"

He grabbed the girl and held a knife to her throat. "You'll both keep quiet and come with me."

He walked them to the Circle, and led them inside near the Portal stones. Xantara tried to pull her daughter away, but he punched her chin, and she fell into a heap.

The knife cut into the girl's neck, releasing a thin trickle of blood. He pointed to a flat stone. "Is this the exact spot they resurrected you?"

Her eyelids fluttered.

Jeremiah had followed them to the circle. He saw Xantara fall to the ground and the man force Imogene onto the stone. The man raised his hand and the moonlight flashed against metal.

No! He couldn't let any harm come to Xantara or Imogene yet. He lifted the army-issue pistol, and fired. A small hole appeared in the middle of the man's forehead, and he fell. Jeremiah rushed forward and grabbed the girl.

Xantara struggled to her feet. "Jeremiah! Don't you hurt my child."

He stared hard and shook his head. "Ezekiel said she had been resurrected. It proves you are a witch!"

"As I told you, it's the Guardians who heal."

"Yes, and that's why I'm here. I've discovered that we are cousins. That's why we look alike, and we are both Albinos. If you can be healed, then so can I. I deserve it the same as you."

Xantara stepped back. "Cousins? How can we be? My father was an only child, and I have no cousins!"

"My father raped your aunt Sybil when she was a teen," he said. "She obviously didn't tell anyone, went away for the birth, and left me at the home for unwed mothers to be adopted. My father adopted me, then raised me with Ezekiel and two brothers."

Xantara glared at him. "If we're related, then so are you and Imogene. Please, please, let her go."

Jeremiah smiled. "I will if you help me."

"I'll do anything. What do you want?"

"My eyes are failing. I want you to heal them, as yours have been."

A tear ran down her cheek. "I can't. The time must be right, and eight Guardians must be present to release the full power."

"I don't believe you. You're just playing for time. Do it now, or I'll twist her head off."

Xantara grabbed for her daughter, but he yanked the child back out of her reach. Imogene tried to speak, and he relaxed his grip on her neck.

"Don't hurt Mommy! I'll heal your sight."

"You? But how can you do it?"

"I became a Light Being for a time while I was dead, and now I have healing powers. Promise to let us go, and I'll try."

"Okay, do it now. Xantara, you keep back. Let's see what she can do. If she heals me, I'll let you both go."

Xantara moved away, and he turned the girl around. "Right. One chance. Heal me, and I promise not to harm you or your mother."

Heat infused him as Imogene placed her hands over his eyes. He became hotter and hotter, and cried out. She lifted her hands, stepped back, and waited. He staggered, looked around, but everything was still blurred. Then, gradually, his sight cleared, and he could see perfectly. She'd healed him!

Xantara rushed forward and grabbed Imogene's hand. They ran off, and he raised his gun. Ezekiel would be happy if he killed them both. He aimed...

Braeden raced past the stones. "Xantara, Imogene, where are you?"

His blood ran cold as he entered the circle. His wife and daughter ran toward him, chased by a man with a gun. "Put the gun down - police officers are right behind me," he called.

The man hesitated, and Braeden shouted again. "Police! Over here!"

The man's hand dropped, and he turned and ran off into the dark. The spinning of a motorcycle's wheels sounded in the distance as it sped away.

Braeden sighed with relief. "Are you all right?"

They fell into his arms and sobbed. Xantara broke free from his embrace. "Where are the police?"

"There aren't any. I had to do something to scare him off."

His wife pointed to a body. "We'll have to call them. He killed a man."

Braeden walked them back to Bryony's house, hid Imogene upstairs, and phoned the police.

Detective McCullage got up and dressed hurriedly. These late-night call-outs played havoc with his body clock. What now?

He walked into Avebury circle, toward the lights and commotion. A police officer blinded him with his flashlight. "Sorry, sir. The body's over here."

The man lay on his back, a neat hole through his forehead. McCullage took the flashlight from the officer and played its beam over the man's face. "Henry Wall, the psychopath. Wasn't he transferred to Dartmoor prison today?"

The officer cleared his throat. "He escaped, after killing the escort guards."

McCullage shrugged. "No loss to society, but a shame about the guards. Get the forensics team down here. I'll go interview the Pembrokes again."

The officer directed him to Bryony's house. "It's within walking distance."

He set off. What was it with this family? And now he had to tell them about their daughter's mislaid body. Not a pleasant task.

~ *** ~

He knocked, and Braeden opened the door. "Come in."

McCullage sat opposite the white-faced couple. "Before we talk about the murdered man, there's another matter to discuss." He stared at his own hands, flexing his fingers several times, and looked up.

"I'm sorry to have to tell you, but your daughter's body is missing from the mortuary. We've checked the security cameras, but found no footage to tell us what happened."

Braeden clasped his hands together. "I have to confess. I did it. We brought her here to the Stones, a group of us performed a ceremony, and she came back to life! She's here now."

McCullage looked around room. "You've got to be kidding me! If she's alive, where is she? Is this another of your tricks? Stop this tomfoolery and tell me the truth."

Now they were both crazy. He'd had enough of this. What were they up to?

Xantara stood. "I'll brew a pot of tea."

McCullage looked hard at Braeden. "Don't be ridiculous. If she's alive, let me see her."

Braeden walked into the hallway and called up the stairs. "Imogene! Come down, please."

The young girl entered the room, and the detective went light-headed. It looked like her, but perhaps it was a trick. Maybe he was still asleep, and it was all a dream? "What's your name?" he asked.

"Imogene Pembroke."

He looked at Braeden. "Can you prove it?"

Braeden picked up a photo album from the sideboard and opened it. Together they studied the pictures. "Who's this auburn-haired woman?" the detective asked.

Imogene walked over. "That's Aunty Bryony. This is her house."

McCullage rubbed his eyes and looked at the girl again. He held up the album next to her face. "Do you have a twin?"

"No, but Granny has a twin. Aunt Sybil."

Xantara returned with a tea tray, and set it on the coffee-table. They sat in silence as she poured them each a cup. "Sugar?"

McCullage put the album down. "Three, please. Okay, let's talk about the murder. Do you know the man, or who shot him?"

"The man forced us to walk to the circle, and threatened to kill Imogene if we didn't keep quiet. He started to cut her throat, and the other man shot him."

186

"Did you see who did it?"

"Yes! Jeremiah Yates, the cousin of Ezekiel. He's the fugitive I told you about, the one who stayed in the crypt for a time."

"Why did he do it?"

"I'm sorry, but I have no idea."

The detective stood. "It's late. I'll be back tomorrow with the Inspector. No one's to leave this house. Understood?"

He returned to the murder site and, arms crossed, stared at it. He shook his head to clear it, but couldn't make sense of any of it.

 ***

Azazel drifted over the scene. Failed! Now he'd have to find another body, and try again. He passed through the dimensional veil, and crawled into the cave to face his master.

CHAPTER THIRTY

Hamish McGregor swallowed a mouthful of buttered kipper and looked out the window. In the distance he made out a dust ball bowling toward the Manor. He squinted. Who could it be?

He wiped his mouth, and stood. "Come on, Rex. Let's see who they are."

The Golden Retriever trotted at his side as Hamish went to the front door and picked up binoculars off the hall table. Damn, it looked like an army vehicle. His joints hurt as he walked outside. Couldn't they leave an eighty-two year soul in peace? He loathed interruptions.

The army Land Rover swept into the circular drive, and stopped opposite the front door. Five men in army fatigues got out.

"What do you think you're doing? Get off my property!"

The biggest soldier removed his hat, and he recognized him.

"Ezekiel! What a surprise! How pleasant to see you, come in, come in."

The men trailed in, sat at the breakfast table, and immediately helped themselves to his leftovers. Ezekiel lifted the silver lid and picked out a kipper.

"I'll tell the cook to bring more food." Hamish walked through the hallway toward the back kitchen and stopped outside the scullery door. He leant against the jamb and closed his eyes. Trouble. Must be. He was too old for this.

"Abigail, Ezekiel and his family have turned up. Can you cook them breakfast?"

She picked up a skillet and a tray of eggs. "You mean the owner?"

"Yes, and they're trouble, I'm sure of it."

Hamish returned to the breakfast room and joined them at the table. "Breakfast shouldn't be long. Help yourself to tea. Good to see you, Ezekiel. And if I'm not mistaken, this must be your three cousins. Who're the young men?"

"Malachi's sons. Riordan and Sean, all the way from Dublin."

"Welcome. What brings you to Scotland?"

He watched Ezekiel walk over to the corner television and switch to the news channel. The newscast showed video of Stonehenge, the camera panning round the piles of bodies, their faces blurred for privacy.

A cold chill washed over Hamish. "You did this?"

"Don't look so shocked. You know our father's views. He'd be proud, our wiping out thousands of sinners with a push of a button."

Beads of icy sweat ran down Hamish's face. "I don't think he meant you to go this far."

"Early days, yet! We have far grander plans in mind."

Hamish turned away. "I don't like this. I'll chase up your breakfast."

Hamish wiped his face as he hurried back to the kitchen. Abigail looked up as he opened the kitchen door. "Whatever's the matter?"

"I told you they'd be trouble. But even I can't believe how much. Now I'm involved."

"Weren't you friends with Ezekiel's father?"

"Yes, he asked me to be the Manor caretaker. The Crazy coot's gone now, but the four boys he raised are ten times worse. They blew up Stonehenge!"

Abigail drew in a sharp breath. "I saw it on the news. Thousands killed and injured! The police must be on their trail."

"We'll have to look after them, and if there's a chance, we'll notify the authorities. I'm not off to prison at my age. It'd kill me."

Hamish picked up a couple of dishes. "I'll help you carry them through."

Jim McCullage sat at his desk early the next morning, chewing the end of his pen. He couldn't charge the girl's parents for abducting their own child. Anyway, with the Stonehenge case on his hands, the senior detective wouldn't be interested, so it wouldn't be important. He'd better get on with his reports. The priority was the underground city case notes, then the murder from last night.

As McCullage detailed the discovery of the three bodies and cache of ball-bearings in his report, a persistent ring interrupted him. He continued to write as he picked up the phone.

"Detective McCullage."

A deep voice with an American accent answered. "Good morning. Sam Blackbridge, CIA, from New York."

McCullage frowned. "How can I help you?"

"I'm looking for a missing felon, Jeremiah Yates, who's wanted for an attempted bank robbery. I have reason to believe he's in your area."

McCullage put his pen down and swapped the receiver into his right hand. "I read the New York Times article. Is a relative Ezekiel Yates?"

"Yes. Do you know his family?"

"They're prime suspects in the Stonehenge massacre."

He heard Sam Blackbridge's sharp intake of breath.

"I'm not surprised. He leads the Phineas Priesthood here in New York, and we've been after him for some time. They've committed some violent crimes, but this is the worst we've heard of. I think I'd better come over there."

"I could do with any assistance I can get, see you when you get here."

He hung up. Good. This whole situation tested his experience, and any added expertise would help. He'd better go brief the Home Office team.

Jeremiah ditched the motorbike and walked to the Bristol train station. He caught an overnighter to Aberdeen and crashed on the bunk. The rush of adrenalin from his escape made sleep difficult. He sat up and looked at his reflection in the train car's mirror. Wow! At last his vision was clear. His eyes matched Xantara's exactly, greens and blues, iridescent. He liked the look, but what could this mean? Did the Devil heal him?

Ezekiel met him at the station. His cousin noticed his new eye pigmentation straight away, and questioned him on it. Not much got past Ezekiel.

"I caught up with Xantara and her daughter at Avebury Circle," he said. "The girl healed me. I tried to kill them both, but the husband and police stopped me. I only just got away!"

"You went to the Circle and let the Devil mess with you?"

"God healed me! He can use any vessel. After all, he created the universe."

Ezekiel nodded. "Perhaps that was God's plan. Well, I'm glad your eyes work again. Don't worry about the Pembrokes, we can deal with them later. For now, we must regroup and keep a low profile. You'll enjoy the Manor. You can fish and shoot from dawn to dusk."

McCullage reported to Inspector Grant.

"A CIA agent is on his way from New York," he said. "He believes some religious fanatics could be behind the bombing." He told him about the Phineas Priesthood.

"I've never heard of that cult," Inspector Grant said. "But a terrorist is a terrorist, whatever his motivation. I've asked Senior Detective Swanson if I can borrow you for a while, as your cases seem to all be tied in with this one. I know you'll be a valuable team member."

"Thank you, sir. I'll do my best, of course."

McCullage went to Senior Detective Swanson's office. His boss grimaced as he entered the room. "Jim, I'm busy, and I'll be busier still when you join the Home Office team."

"Sorry, sir, but my information may relate to last night's murder case. Mrs. Pembroke's daughter's body disappeared from the mortuary. I found out that her father took it, and now she's alive. Weird, I know, but I promise you it's true. I've seen her."

"Are you sure it's the same girl?

"Absolutely."

Well, let's go and see, shall we? I have the press on my back, and could do with a breather."

McCullage rapped on the door, and a young auburn-haired woman answered. He recognized her as Bryony, the woman pictured in the album the night before.

She stepped back. "Please come in, everyone's here."

Mr. and Mrs. Pembroke sat either side of Imogene on the settee. "This is Senior Detective Swanson."

Braeden stood and held out his hand. "Detective, please take a seat."

Without a word, McCullage picked up the photo album and passed the pictures to his boss. Swanson studied them and the child. "It certainly seems to be the same girl. We'll have to run DNA tests, of course, to be sure. I don't know how it's possible. Perhaps a deep coma, who knows? I'm sure there's a logical explanation."

Braeden leant forward. "There've been accounts—many accounts, in fact—of people coming back to life. You know, in the Bible and in the present-day."

Swanson coughed. "I'm sure there are. But I'm under a lot of pressure, and would like to keep this low key. We don't want the press sniffing around. It's just the sort of sensational story they'd love."

Mrs. Pembroke visibly relaxed. "We'll stay here a few more days. The press heard about the incident on the island, and we want to avoid them."

McCullage stood. "Before we leave, can you tell me anything more about Jeremiah Yates?"

"I don't think so. My statement covered everything. If I remember any more, I'll call you."

Swanson stood, glanced over at Imogene, and shook his head. "We'll be in touch."

McCullage followed him outside and his boss pulled the car door open. "Funny business. It might be best to let it all stand for the time being. But later, when we have time, we'll investigate it all thoroughly. I still think the family's hiding something."

"Yes, sir. Maybe you're right."

CHAPTER THIRTY-ONE

Sally Lyons peddled furiously toward The Piper's Lament Hotel. She daren't be late, or her first job might be her last. She heard a horn behind her and turned. An old army Land Rover painted black and green bumped her back wheel. She bent low and peddled harder. The car came up alongside and forced her into the ditch.

She flew over the handlebars into the bushes. Dazed, she heard the car brakes squeal. Thank God she'd remembered to wear her helmet. Idiot! No consideration for other road users!

Before she could move, two men hauled her up. A third stuck duct tape over her mouth, then slipped a sack over her head. My, God, they were kidnappers!

She struggled, to no avail. They wrapped more tape around her wrists and ankles and lifted her into the Jeep. She struggled. Would they kill her?

They drove for hours before they stopped the Jeep, then dragged her out. They removed the sack and she looked around, and gasped. A large mansion stood before her, three stories high. They carried her inside, through a long hallway, and three flights up the back stairs.

They took her into a bedroom, removed the tape, and left. Large sash windows draped with dark-green velvet curtains stood on her right. The sparse furniture consisted of a heavy oaken bed made up with a cream quilt and a single pillow, and a modest nightstand next to it.

She ran to the door and yanked the knob. Locked! She tried to open the window, but it didn't budge. She stared out across fields covered with white heather and yellow gorse, which stretched for miles until they met high distant mountains. Trapped, and no one knew her whereabouts. She sat on the bed, shoulders hunched, and waited.

The sun went down, and the room darkened. She needed food and water. Her fists pummeled the door, but no one came. She lay back down and stared at the ceiling, tears flowing down her cheeks. She'd lose her job for sure, and her mother would be worried stiff.

Jeremiah lifted a Waterford crystal tumbler filled with a single malt whisky. "To the Phineas Priesthood."

The others clinked glasses. "The Priesthood."

Hamish McGregor cleared the dishes and topped up the drinks. "What's the young woman here for?"

Jeremiah patted Hamish's arm. "Our fathers did their duty, and now we'll do ours. Think of it, there're six of us, and we have no means of increasing our numbers unless we provide mothers for our children. This is just the start. If we father ten children each, that's sixty home-grown little Phineas Priests. Long-term, I grant you, but think of God's approval when we advance His agenda." Jeremiah sipped his drink and sat back down.

After dinner, Obadiah tuned to the news channel. The blast at Stonehenge dominated the news. So far the government hadn't assigned blame, and no one claimed responsibility. "I can't see how they can connect us, unless they clear the tunnel and discover we're not dead," he said. "Excavation would take months, and even then no one can track us here."

Ezekiel passed the port around. "You'll see. God protects His own."

The others went to bed, and Jeremiah said he would be up later. He bypassed the first floor and continued up the second set of stairs to the attic.

He unlocked the young woman's bedroom door, stepped inside, and relocked it behind him. She sat up and stared at him, a look of horror on her face.

"Hello my dear."

~ *** ~

Azazel cowered before his master. "It wasn't my fault. Who's Jeremiah's controller, and why didn't he stop him?"

The master's three horns quivered. "You're pathetic! I've warned you, if the girl delivers her message, we'll lose millions of souls. What do you intend to do?"

"Master, I need to use someone close to her, but she's surrounded by sealed souls. I can't possess them."

"Don't give me your pitiful excuses. Find someone."

Azazel bowed low and inched backwards. "I'll stop her, master. I promise."

~ *** ~

Sam Blackbridge walked into the police station's incident room and gave a mock bow. "CIA, at your service."

McCullage walked over, smiled, and shook his hand. "Pleased to meet you, and welcome to the UK."

The man's forthright manner suited his slicked black hair and warm brown eyes. He could have walked fresh off "The Men in Black" film set. McCullage called Inspector Grant over, and introduced them. They shook hands, and the Home Office team gathered around.

Sam opened his briefcase and set out his files. "The Phineas Priesthood is a serious problem for the United States government," he said, "and we believe Jeremiah Yates will try to set up a chapter here. He's responsible for multiple robberies and at least two murders."

McCullage briefed him on the Yates family. "At first we believed they perished in the collapsed tunnel, but recent findings contradict that," he said. "The investigation points toward their involvement in the Stonehenge massacre. We have no idea where they've disappeared to."

Sam looked up from his file. "I have to warn you, the Priesthood causes havoc in America, and now your home-grown chapter will stop at nothing."

As the meeting closed McCullage tapped Sam's shoulder. "Fancy dinner and a pint down at our local?"

"Sounds good to me."

At the pub, McCullage ordered two beef curries and two lagers, paid, and joined Sam at the corner table. They exchanged a few jokes, then Jim told him about the Pembroke's bizarre events.

Sam downed his drink. "I've heard of people brought back to life, mainly Southern Baptists. On occasion the church has claimed to have such answers to prayer, but usually they occurred only a few hours after death, I believe. But as they say, there's more mystery in heaven and earth. I like to keep an open mind, and would love to meet her."

"I'll see what I can do. Another?"

Xantara stood at the door, holding Imogene's hand. "Thank you for your kindness, Bryony. You're such a treasured friend."

Bryony hugged them both. "You're welcome to stay as long as you like. But perhaps old routines would be best."

As soon as Xantara parked the car at the clinic, Imogene jumped out. "Come on, Mom, I want to play school. Will you play with me?"

Xantara laughed, and they went upstairs. A half hour later, Imogene's dolls and stuffed animals dutifully sat in a line. "Pay attention, children. Today we'll learn the 'three times' table."

Warmth filled Xantara's heart. How she'd missed these magical moments! An unexpected cold chill ran through her. What did the future hold? And what was the message?

Cameraman Hugh Grantham stowed his gear into the Channel Five van. He'd seen enough gore to last a lifetime, and wished he could leave Stonehenge for good. His team awaited further orders, and they couldn't come too soon. He turned to Susanna Prentice, the anchor.

"You okay?"

The slender blonde flicked her hair back and smiled. "I've been better. It makes you think about your own mortality, doesn't it?"

"Sure does. I don't know, but I've heard rumors about a young girl miraculously brought back to life."

A cloud covered the sun, and Hugh zipped his blue bomber jacket. He preferred Spain to the English summer.

"I hope there's a smidgeon truth in it. We need a feel-good story after this. Come on, let's go back to our digs, get a drink, and eat dinner. We can quiz the locals there about the girl."

Hugh pulled up outside The Cockerel in Monkton St Michael. He'd been grateful to get the last two rooms available for miles. The world's press had descended on Stonehenge, and this was the nearest village with empty rooms.

He washed up, then joined Susanna in the snug. The locals jostled at the bar as they waited for the harassed bartender to serve them. He pushed his way through them.

"Two glasses of white wine, please. What's all the excitement about?"

The bartender passed over the drinks. "I'll add it to your tab. A local girl, the doctor's daughter. We attended her funeral over two weeks ago, but someone just saw her walk from her parent's car into the clinic."

"So, there's truth to the rumor, then?"

"Her comeback is a fact. At least five people have seen her so far."

Hugh returned to the table and handed Susanna her wine. "Hey, the miracle girl may be true. Our luck's in! She's here in the village, and lives behind the High Street clinic."

Susanna beamed. "Well done! Let's see if we can get an exclusive."

Hugh led her around the corner, into the High Street. The clinic's upstairs window glowed behind drawn curtains.

Susanna banged the door. No answer. She knocked louder. The light went out.

"We'll return tomorrow, the child will be in bed." She gave a little skip. "Hugh, I'm so excited! This could be my chance for a worldwide scoop.   And   where   I   go   you   go,   too!"

CHAPTER THIRTY-TWO

Kabshiel and the Council of Elders looked deep into the marble scrying bowl. "Out of all the billions of galaxies and planets, Earth is the most troublesome," he said.

They watched black men, dressed in an assortment of army fatigues and black clothing, enter a Nigerian shopping mall. Their leader raised his gun and shot a white woman who stood out among the predominately black shoppers at point-blank range. More shots rang out as they targeted each white or foreign face. The shoppers screamed and ducked for cover.

The assassins herded a group into the cafeteria corner, and one by pulled them forward.

"Recite a Muslim prayer," the leader said.

A young mother, with babe in arms and her face half-covered, trembled. "God is the greatest. God is the greatest. I bear witness that there is none worthy of worship but God. I bear witness that Muhammad is the prophet of God".

The gunman waved his pistol. "You can go. Next."

A mature black couple with greying hair moved forward. "Please let us go. We're Christians, but do no harm."

He shot them both in the head, and moved on. Shrieks rang out as the gunman closed in, shooting anyone in sight.

Another assassin walked into the baby store and found a young couple hidden behind the counter, the woman visibly pregnant. Her pale face, framed by light blonde hair, exploded with one shot. He aimed at her husband. "You can join her, may Allah be praised."

The Elders watched as body after body dropped, and soul after soul rose. Kabshiel waved over the scrying bowl, it's water stilled. "Let's move on." The water swirled, and the African massacre image gave way to a Middle Eastern setting.

The small child coughed as his father poured water over his head. Sarin gas fumes filled his throat. His daughter and wife lay behind him. They'd succumbed quickly, but his son still lived. Two rows of white-sheeted bodies lay across the room, and others were being carried in.

"Come on, son, breathe. You can do it!" The small child's eyelids closed. "Allah, help me, don't let my son die!"

Kabshiel waved again, and the Elders looked down on an American Navy base. The crazed, armed killer shot staff indiscriminately. Each short report felled another soul.

"This has to stop. We must deliver the message," Kabshiel said. The image faded, and the Elders sat down. "Call Rahmiel. The time has come."

Azazel hovered over the clinic. Time grew short, and he needed to find someone close to the girl, someone with a chink in their soul. He probed the mind of a farmer in the waiting room. Too pure. He delved into another patient's mind, then another. The people weren't perfect, but weren't corrupt enough to allow possession. He tried the nurse receptionist. Now she interested him!

Hilda Moore changed the old man's dressings. "There David, you'll be more comfortable. Have you spoken to your lawyer about those papers yet?"

"Yes, he dropped them off for me to sign yesterday."

"Where are they? Have you signed them?"

The old man rummaged in his dressing-gown pocket and pulled out a crumpled envelope. "Here, all signed. Thank you for offering to be my power of attorney. I don't know what I'd have done, with the family gone."

Hilda snatched the papers from him and stuffed them in her apron pocket. "No problem, David. When the time comes, years from now I'm sure, I'll take care of your estate and carry out your wishes to the letter." She released his wheelchair's brakes and pushed him back to his room and helped him to bed. "I'll come back later with your medication. Rest a while."

An hour later, after the hallway lights dimmed, Hilda went into the dispensary and picked up a syringe and vial. They should do the trick. The old man was frail, so the dose should be enough. She crept along the corridor and slipped into his room. Good, he was asleep. He didn't stir as she slid the needle into a vein and depressed the plunger. She smiled. Another few thousand would top off her bank account nicely.

Unnoticed, Azazel merged his energy with hers. He grinned. This would please his master. This woman saw the child every day. Perfect!

Xantara made sandwiches for lunch, and Imogene set the table. "What shall we do for your birthday tomorrow?"

Imogene put her finger to her cheek, and frowned. "Let's have a picnic at Avebury Circle. We can ask Aunty Bryony to go, too."

"Excellent idea, and you can take a ball to play with Daddy. I'll bake your cake this afternoon."

"Thanks. I want eight candles to blow out, and lots of presents. And lots of people."

Xantara finished the sandwiches and sat down. "Sorry, sweetie, but we can't ask many people, with the press on the prowl. Granny, and Aunt Sybil, of course, and I expect Hilda would like to come. Would you help me mix your birthday cake?"

"Yes, please. Oh, I can't wait till tomorrow!"

Anchor-woman Susanna Prentice tottered down High Street, her high heels clicking with every step. Hugh held her elbow to keep her upright.

"Do you think the word's gotten out yet?" he asked.

She reached the clinic door. "I hope not. This article's my big chance." The bell tinkled as she pushed the door open.

A grey-haired nurse with a lived-in appearance barred her way. Her name tag said "Hilda."

"Good morning. How can I help you?"

"I'd like to talk to Imogene and her parents, please."

"May I ask what for?"

"The villagers say the girl died, and miraculously came back to life."

"What rubbish! Leave me your card, and I'll ask Doctor Pembroke to ring you."

Susanna tried to look around the nurse. "A few minutes, please?"

The nurse moved forward. "What part of 'no' don't you understand?"

The TV anchor backed off and went outside. She held Hugh's arm, and they made their way back to the pub. She turned to him. "Did you see her eyes? They were dead, dark as a moonless night."

Rahmiel bowed before the Council of Elders. "Greetings, I'm at your service."

"Please sit," Kabshiel said. "Rahmiel, it's time for Imogene to deliver her message. We're dismayed at the escalation of violence on Earth. Mankind will be a race of soulless beasts in less than a generation, unless we act now."

"The girl's strong, and well-suited to be our vessel. Give me the message and I'll see that she delivers it."

Rahmiel committed the words to memory, bowed, and left. Now it was time to check on Imogene. She enjoyed the assignment. The girl was delightful, but the task great.

She appeared in Imogene's bedroom. The girl, lying in bed reading, looked up. "I waited for you. Will you stay and visit a while?"

Rahmiel smiled and perched on the end of her bed. "Tomorrow's a big day."

"Yes, it's my birthday. I'm eight. We're having a picnic at Avebury. Would you like to come?"

"Happy birthday! Yes, I'll be there. Tomorrow's the day to deliver the Council's message. Don't be afraid. I'll speak through you. The sensation may seem a little strange, but you'll be fine."

Imogene yawned. "What a wonderful day it'll be. I can't wait!"

The next morning Susanna sat in the mobile media van with Hugh. She yawned. "I'm bored. Stonehenge is almost cleared, and our job here is done. I'll have a walk around and catch up with the other reporters."

She walked up behind the BBC group, stopped and listened. Oh no, they were discussing Imogene. "I've heard the girl's birthday party is in Avebury Circle, today," one said.

The word was out!

She raced back to Hugh. "Come on, they all know. Get the crew together."

CHAPTER THIRTY-THREE

Braeden spread out the tartan picnic rug. What a glorious day!

"Come on, Imogene. We'll play ball while Mom, Sabina and Sybil unpack the food. Bryony and Hilda can form a team and play with us."

He threw the ball to Imogene and Bryony made a half-hearted attempt to block her.

~ *** ~

Hilda Moore watched them a few moments, then opened her bag and produced a small bright pink cake, shaped like a number eight. "Xantara, look, I made this is for Imogene. It's a special cake, for a special girl."

"Thank you, you're kind. And thank you for fending off those television people yesterday. Braeden and I don't know how we'd manage without you."

Azazel mentally nudged Hilda. "That rock to the left there—isn't that where Imogene came back to life? I still can't believe we have her back!"

Imogene bounded over and saw the two cakes. "Mom, can I eat the small cake now, then blow out the candles on ours later?"

"Yes, Sweetie, but don't eat too much, and thank Hilda. She made it."

"Thank you, Hilda."

Hilda hugged her. "You're welcome." She cut a piece, handed it to Imogene, and pointed to the rock. "Let's take it over there. I want to whisper a secret to you."

Arms around each other, they walked to the stone and sat. Imogene raised the cake to her mouth. "What's the secret?"

Azazel smiled. Good. His plan was working.

Then he sensed a presence. Rahmiel!

"No you don't!" Rahmiel waved her hand, and a gust of wind rose up, so fierce that it blew Imogene's dress up in the air. She dropped the cake into the dirt as she held her dress down.

The evil entity bared his teeth. "I'm not done yet."

The rumble of engines approached, and Braeden looked up. They got closer, bringing the smell of diesel. Media trucks pulled up and surrounded the circle. The wagon train halted, and people jumped from the vans and swarmed into the circle.

"Can't we even have a birthday party in peace?" he called to them.

He glanced at Imogene, still sitting on the stone with Hilda. Damn the press. They were well named, they pressed him in on every side. Microphones sprouted under his nose as he tried to reach Imogene.

Reporters fought to get closer. "What can you tell us about your daughter? Is it true she was buried and came back to life?"

Braeden looked for Xantara. They'd trampled the picnic food into the grass, and she frantically tried to clear the mess up. The World's press must have heard and moved as one body from Stonehenge to Avebury Circle.

He tried again to reach Imogene, who now stood on the stone, looking around. Her face looked radiant and a soft glow pulsated around her body. What was going on?

The light became more pronounced, and the crowd turned. A silence descended over the circle. His nurse Hilda looked wildly around, then her gaze fixed back on Imogene. She yelled, and her teeth bared as she pulled a knife from her pocket and grabbed the girl.

As she raised the knife, a photographer's camera flashed in her face, momentarily blinding her. Another knocked her away and disarmed her. Braeden gasped. Did his nurse just try to kill his daughter? Thank God for reporters!

The glow around his child pulsed faster, and Imogene gently rose off the stone. The crowd gasped as she floated higher, then stopped just over their heads. Flashbulbs popped as the photographers bombarded his daughter. A cameraman shoved him aside and zeroed in on her face.

"Impossible!" a reporter shouted. The light around Imogene strengthened. The crowd froze, every eye focused on her.

Imogene spoke. Her voice sounded mature, with the timbre of a woman.

"I am Rahmiel, a Light Being from the stars. I have a message for all humankind, from the Universal Creator, and Spiritual Masters. People of Earth, you've failed in your search for your life purpose. The World's a classroom, and your lives were given to help you learn these lessons. They encompass the growth of love, grace, humility, mercy and compassion, faith and hope. Your progress is miserable on all counts. Today some of your newly born infants have no souls. Psychopathic behavior, murder, extortion, and extreme brutality, have all increased. These individuals commit these crimes without fear or compassion, for they have no souls.

"Although many people have developed higher abilities, few use them. These should be used, especially intuitive power, for the good of mankind. Your conscience and intuition guide you daily, but you ignore their promptings.

"You expect favors in return for the smallest kindness, instead of helping for the joy of it. Give generously to all in need, and expect nothing in return. One of life's greatest lessons is unselfishness.

Only The Creator has power over life or death. Consider the starving millions who die each day because of self-interest by the authorities who divert relief efforts to purchase weapons. The wars caused by discontent, greed, desire for power. Governments want to take and accumulate wealth instead of serving.

"Only the Creator can pass judgment, yet you judge, all of you. The cause of the World's problems is the extreme prejudice you inflict on your fellow man. Religion is pitted against religion, black against white, rich against poor. You discriminate against homosexuality, the disabled, anyone who is 'different.'

Your prejudices have resulted in millions of soulless children. Countless deaths, murders, destruction of people and property, are the consequence. Your present course will destroy the planet if not checked in time.

"Unless the world addresses these problems, the soulless children will increase. You are creating your own psychopaths, sociopaths, murderers and terrorists. Do any of you want the next generation to be completely soulless?

"World leaders must communicate with one another and broker peace. You must destroy evil weapons of all kinds, or you will face extreme consequences.

World leaders, beware. Your progress will be monitored.

Take heed, this is your last chance. You have been warned!"

CHAPTER THIRTY-FOUR

As Imogene finished her speech, Braeden glanced around. The world's press stood silently, stunned. He looked back as she gently descended, then pandemonium broke out. Everyone surged forward, toward his defenceless little girl. He must get to her. The noise rose about him like the sound of an oversized hive of angry bees.

He dashed toward her, but the media blocked his path. He elbowed them aside, but more came, then a brawny cameraman helped him through. Braeden recognised him as the one who'd saved Imogene earlier from his crazy nurse. The woman with him defended his other side, and he reached his daughter.

The cameraman pointed towards the Channel Five media van. Carrying Imogene, Braeden dashed towards it. They all piled in and locked the doors. The crowd pounded the van as the cameraman pressed the accelerator and the media scattered.

Braeden clung to his daughter. "Thank you, that was close."

The cameraman swerved around a corner. "You're welcome. My name's Hugh, and this is Susanna. Where shall we go?"

"We have a good friend close by." He directed Hugh to Bryony's house. "Park around the back, she won't mind."

The van stopped, and Braeden ran to the house. He pulled the key from under the flowerpot, opened the door, and motioned toward the couch. They all sat. He took in a deep breath and exhaled it slowly. "Bryony and my family are still there," he said. "I hope they can get home."

~ *** ~

Xantara Pembroke led Bryony, Sabina, and Sybil away from the crowd of reporters, and they slipped behind a rock and skirted the circle towards Bryony's house. Imogene ran to meet her mother as she stepped inside. "Are you all right, Mommy?"

Xantara hugged her. "Never mind me, are you okay?"

"I'm fine, Mom. Rahmiel wouldn't hurt me. She warned me first, so I expected it."

Reporter Susanna approached quickly, her voice recorder in hand. "Who's Rahmiel?"

Xantara exchanged glances with her husband. "It's a long story," she said, "and hard to believe. You saved Imogene's life—let me catch my breath, and I'll tell you."

Bryony closed the curtains and switched on the lamps. "Would anyone like tea?" They all nodded, and she went into the kitchen.

Xantara followed her. "What do you think? Should we tell them the whole story? They are the media, after all."

Bryony poured boiling water into the teapot. "You'll have to talk to them eventually. Why not try for an exclusive deal with Channel Five, and let them liaise with the other networks? That way you'll avoid being hassled."

"Good idea. Thanks." Xantara picked up the tray.

She returned to the living room and explained the plan. Susanna beamed. "Thank you so much. We won't let you down, and we'll keep the other news hounds at bay."

"You're welcome. Come back tomorrow, and we'll talk. Imogene must rest, and we need to collect our thoughts."

~ *** ~

Home Secretary Alexander Brittan crashed through the door, and Frank Carrington looked up. "What's wrong, Alex?"

"Switch the television on."

He did, and they watched footage of a child giving a speech as she floated several feet in the air. He changed channels and watched the same scene again. "It has to be a hoax."

"The world's media witnessed the incident," Brittan said. "That footage has gone viral. They say the girl died, then came back to life."

Frank's eyebrows went up. "Really?"

"Really. Detective Jim McCullage at the Swindon constabulary confirmed the story."

"Where is that?"

"Avebury Circle, an ancient stone circle near Stonehenge." Brittan shook his head. "A terrorist attack, and now this! A Home Office team is already in Wiltshire. Call the commander and tell him to find the girl and take her and anyone with her into custody for their own safety."

"Shall I order the car brought round for us, sir?"

Inspector Grant replaced the phone. "McCullage, where's this girl likely to be?"

The detective frowned. "They wouldn't go back home. They have a friend, Bryony, who lives a short walk from Avebury Circle. She hid out there after the resurrection."

"Resurrection. That's downright…well, get out to the house and check. I want them all in custody."

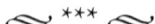

Ezekiel felt his blood boil as he watched Imogene descend onto the stone. He switched channels. Her image haunted him as he clicked through more channels. "That wretched girl! Look, the Devil controls her now. I need to consult The Lord about this."

He went to his room and knelt beside the bed. "Lord, hear my prayer. The girl is now the Devil's puppet. What would you have me do?"

Calmness came over him as he waited.

"Son, my faithful servant, there is more to be done. Take Jeremiah, Riordan and Sean with you. Jeremiah knows the house in which she resides. For her death to be permanent, you must kill her within Avebury Circle."

A half an hour later, the men drove the Land Rover over the Scottish border and headed for Wiltshire.

Ezekiel led his crew around the back, and he saw that the house was quiet and the curtains were drawn. Jeremiah crashed his shoulder against the rear door and it burst open. A woman inside screamed. Braeden rushed into the kitchen, and Riordan snatched up a wooden rolling pin and smashed it against the doctor's head. He dropped to the floor and lay still.

The three women were in the lounge. But where was Imogene?

"Round up the women," Ezekiel said, as he made his way upstairs. He opened a bedroom door and peered in. The child lay under the covers, the tip of her nose poking out. He snatched the covers back, and she rolled onto her back and stared at him. "You murderer! You can't hurt me again. I'm protected."

Ezekiel yanked her up by her arm. "We'll see about that, young lady." He dragged her down the stairs and outside, where the others waited with the three women for instructions. "We'll hole up in the church until the Circle's clear."

Malachi's sons put Imogene and Xantara into the Land Rover, and took the others in Bryony's car.

Jim McCullage banged on Bryony's front door. No answer. He walked around the back and found the kitchen door smashed in, and almost tripped as he entered. Braeden Pembroke lay deathly still across the tiles. He checked his pulse, and found it strong. Good. He wet a towel and dabbed the bleeding scull wound. Braeden moaned and opened his eyes. "McCullage, he's taken them."

"Who?"

"Ezekiel and his men have taken them all."

Ezekiel's family paused at the church's door. "Hide the cars," he told Sean. "You others—we're going inside."

Jeremiah caught his arm. "Won't this be the first place they'll look?"

Ezekiel smiled. "That's why it's a perfect hideout. They'll check here first, find it clear, and cross the site off their list. You just watch."

They entered the church, and Ezekiel pressed a carved Tudor rose set in the oak-panelled wall. He slid the panel back to reveal a secret space.

Jeremiah poked his head inside. "What's in there?"

"It's an old priest hole that leads down to the tunnels," Ezekiel said. "Follow me."

He picked up a candle and lit it. Sean came back, and they ushered the women and child into the opening, and told them to turn left. Ezekiel held the candle high, illuminating another entry.

They entered the space one by one and climbed down narrow stone stairs, which opened into a circular room. Five archways in the room led into the tunnels. "Sit," he said, pointing to the rough stone walls. He lit wall rushes with his candle, then lit a cigar and watched the women in silence as he smoked. The smell of the Havana filled the room.

Jeremiah crossed the room, pulled Sybil to her feet, and pressed her against the wall, their noses almost touching. "Mother, dearest. How are you?"

Sybil's face blanched. "Mother? Why do you call me that?"

"Surprise, surprise. Never thought you'd see me again, did you?" He threw her down and spat on her. "How could you leave a helpless baby in an institution? My father came for me and raised me. But you didn't care, did you?"

Sybil shook and covered her face. "I'm sorry, truly sorry."

Not as sorry as you're going to be. I promise you that."

McCullage drove Braeden toward the church. "Do you know how Imogene did it?" he asked.

"Rise up in the air, you mean? To be honest, I don't know anything, anymore. My whole world has turned into a nightmare."

"The Home Office will investigate it. For your sake, I hope you're not pulling some sick joke."

He parked in the church's empty car park. They searched the main building and crypt, inch by inch, and found both empty. The detective noticed a small item near the panelled west wall, and picked it up and turned to Braeden. "Recognize this?"

"Yes, it's Xantara's star necklace. She never takes it off. They have to be close."

"We need help. Let's go back to Swindon and raise a search team."

CHAPTER THIRTY-FIVE

Braeden followed McCullage into the station and headed toward the back rooms. The desk sergeant darted forward and held the door. "Heads up, sir, the Prime Minister and Home Secretary are in the incident room. Inspector Grant has asked for you."

"Thank you, sergeant. Look after Dr Pembroke for me."

Braeden's cell phone played a tune, and he stared at its face. "Sergeant, I have to answer this." He walked outside, and took a deep breath of the fresh air. "Alistair, did you see the news?"

"I did, and drove straight down. Is Imogene okay?"

For some reason, his voice seemed reassuring. "Would you pick me up outside Swindon Constabulary? I'll bring you up to date."

"Sure, I'm two blocks away."

Braeden snapped his phone shut and walked to the corner. In moments Alistair pulled over, and he scrambled into his car.

"Drive to the church. Ezekiel has kidnapped your mother, Imogene, and the others. We found your mother's star necklace on the church floor, with a broken chain."

"Mom always wears it, she must have left it as a clue for us." Alistair sped along the country lanes.

 ***

Inspector Grant frowned. "McCullage, about time. Did you find the girl?"

McCullage shook his head. "She's been abducted, sir. They knocked Dr Pembroke unconscious. I found him, and when he came round we visited the church. It's Ezekiel and his clan again, and they've disappeared."

"That seems to be a habit of his. Would you please update us?

McCullage shook hands all around, and sat facing Frank Carrington. As he went through the known facts, CIA Agent Sam Blackbridge came in, and he introduced him.

Blackbridge stepped forward. "The President is concerned, not only about the terrorists but this girl," he said. "He wants to know if her performance is genuine, and if she's connected in any way with the massacre and the Phineas Priesthood."

Frank Carrington grimaced. "We're as puzzled about the child as everyone else. We think we've identified the terrorists, and their connection to The Phineas Priesthood."

Inspector Grant rapped the board with his pointer. "Sir, I suggest we have the Counter Terrorist Command hunt them down, and find the Pembroke family."

"Get to it, Inspector. I'll call the President."

Jeremiah eyed the group sitting with their backs against the tight room's circular wall, his skin itching from the stuffy atmosphere. He glowered at his mother.

God, he hated her.

"So, mother, what's your excuse? Why did you abandon me?"

Sybil wrung her hands. "It was a different time. In those days, people ostracized rape victims. I was a scared eighteen-year-old girl, and the home wanted me to leave you there for your own good."

Jeremiah's stomach tightened, and his heart filled with hatred. "What did you think when you saw I was an albino?"

"I wasn't surprised. Avebury Village has produced Albinos for generations."

Jeremiah threw a small rock her. "I've despised you all my life, and you will pay for your sins."

Alistair parked near the church door, and he and Braeden got out and entered. A hush hung over the building, and sunlight streamed in through the leaded windows.

Braeden walked to the west wall. "We found your mother's necklace there," he said, pointing. He tapped the wall. The hollow sound echoed around the sanctuary.

Alistair took two solid brass candlesticks from the altar. "These might come in handy. I assume they'll be armed."

Braeden hesitated. "Maybe McCullage is right, and we should wait for backup."

"We may be too late, Dad."

"You're right. We can't risk them being harmed."

As Braeden moved along the aisle, he felt a soft waft of air brush his cheek. That was odd. The church doors were closed. Frowning, he turned slowly, until the cool air hit his face. It seemed to come from the wall itself. He walked along it, and the breeze seemed to change direction. He paused.

There seemed to be a crack between two panels. He felt the separation, and realized one panel was loose. He pulled it toward him and was again hit by the moving air.

Alistair came up behind him. "What are you doing, Dad?"

Braeden gripped the edge and pulled the panel back and looked inside. "There's a passageway down here." He frowned into the near darkness, and made out a stairway to the left. "Light those candles," he said. "We're going exploring."

Kabshiel watched Braeden and Alistair in his scrying bowl, as the Council of Elders stood around him. "They have to be in time! We can't allow Ezekiel to kill the child. We have to keep them from taking her to the Circle."

He waved, and the scene changed. A series of television programmes flashed by, and concerned citizens discussed the phenomenon of her rising from the dead. He stood back and crossed his arms. "The message has reached the entire globe. No man can say they haven't been warned."

Azazel looked out through Ezekiel's eyes. Good, he wouldn't fail this time. His minion Gressil inhabited Jeremiah, and judging by the man's uneasiness, Gressil was stirring up a nasty concoction. He expected the albino man to explode with rage at any moment.

Azazel shot his assistant a mental warning. "Calm down, the time isn't ripe yet."

Susanna and Hugh sat in the van. "I'm so frustrated," she said. "They've tied our hands with the 'Official Secrets' document they made us sign." Her cell phone beeped, and she answered it. "Yes, boss, good news. The girl's family has promised us an exclusive. We'll interview them tomorrow."

Her boss's voice grew louder, then the phone clicked as he disconnected. She jammed it into her purse and turned to Hugh. "He's not happy. He wants us to interview them now, or we're off the job."

Hugh shook his head. "Idiots! They've got no idea what's going on down here."

He started the van and shot off toward the cottage. They pulled around to the back, and Susanna jumped out and paused. She stared at the broken door. "Hugh, we may be too late," she whispered.

They entered the kitchen and she saw the bloodied tiles. "Something's happened here. She stood straight, looking around. "Let's have a little prowl around."

They searched every room on the first floor, and found nothing amiss. Frowning, she left him and went upstairs, and peeked into the bedrooms. She stepped into the master bedroom and glanced about. Again, nothing.

The closet door was cracked open, and on impulse she opened it wider and looked in. A long white robe hung on a padded hanger. How strange. She felt its fabric, and took it from the closet rod. It looked like a Halloween costume. She shut the closet and opened the dressing table drawer. It held assorted vials, none of which looked like perfume. She pulled a stopper and sniffed, and peered at the label. Herbs! This must have a Guardian connection. Xantara had briefly mentioned ceremonies.

She went downstairs. "Hugh, this is the story of a lifetime. I could write a book! Come on, let's track them down."

Susanna needed a change of clothes, and directed Hugh back to Monkton St Michael. As they neared the pub she noticed the church against the skyline, and turned to Hugh. "Isn't that where they buried her? Cemetery footage would be useful."

He nodded, and turned the van toward the church.

Inspector Grant rallied his team. "There are several probable sites to search," he said. "Re-examine the underground city, Ezekiel's house, St Michael's church—I want every inch scrutinized, is that clear?"

He returned to the incident room. "Prime Minister, my men will be meticulous. If there's anything to find, they'll find it. Did you talk to the President?"

Frank sipped his coffee. "Yes, he wants to be kept informed, naturally. The FBI has already examined the girl's CNN footage. They can't find any evidence of trickery."

"What will you do with her? When you find her, of course."

"She needs a complete physical workup and a thorough mental evaluation. We're lucky an eminent psychiatrist with experience with children is nearby."

"Who's that?"

"His name's Ernst Schneider and he's at our military testing complex at Porton Down, on the Salisbury plain."

"Oh! Of course. I've heard of him."

Susanna and Hugh reached the church car park and saw a green Renault near the door. They parked the van alongside it, and Hugh retrieved his camera from the back. "Let's film the gravesite first."

They entered the graveyard, and Susanna studied the weatherworn stones near the entrance. Most were dated more than a hundred years before. She glanced about, and spotted a fresh grave down the hill, near a large oak tree that might have been a sapling when the cemetery was started. It had no headstone, which meant it was dug only a short time before. Beyond the graveyard, a large plain stretched for miles. It was beautiful, and easy to see why the Normans built here so long ago.

Hugh looked about, and spotted the church. "Look at those stunning windows," he said. "What an effective opening shot."

Susanna nodded, and walked toward it. "It is beautiful. Take the pictures, then we'll explore it."

He finished in a few minutes, and they walked to the church. Inside, they explored every room. When they reached the crypt stairs, she stopped. Hadn't Xantara mentioned this? She turned to Hugh, who was taking an art shot of the glowing windows, from low on the floor between pews.

"Let's go down," she said.

He finished his shot and stood, wiping his knees. "Lead on."

They went down the dark stairs, and she walked slowly to the cells. Now, that was unusual. Some cells still held blankets and food. She saw traces of blood around the centre stone.

They went back up into the main church, and Hugh walked around the room, looking for good photo opportunities. As Susanna looked around, a disturbing thought hit her. Whose car was that outside?

"Hello? Anyone here?"

Silence.

Hugh turned to again admire the stained glass, and walked backwards along the wall for a better view. As he did he noticed a panel missing, and a dark opening beyond it.

"Hey Suze, come over here."

Together they looked in. Hugh switched on his camera lights and panned around. "Look, to your left. It's a passageway."

She smiled. This was getting interesting. "Come on, let's explore."

CHAPTER THIRTY-SIX

The candlelight cast a small yellow pool around Braeden and Alistair as they crept down the steps. The doctor heard a scream and ran down the last few steps, to see them all sitting against the circular wall.

Jeremiah leapt to his feet, grabbed Sabina, a held knife to her throat. "Stop right where you are!"

Braeden paused. "Relax, we won't harm you. Let her go." He blew out the flame and lowered the candlestick. "You can't get away with this. They'll catch you, eventually."

Jeremiah grinned. "I've already killed thousands. What's one more? Many husbands would beg me to get rid of their mother-in-law!"

Braeden stepped toward him, and the albino's grip tightened on the knife.

"Come on, she hasn't harmed you."

Jeremiah switched his gaze to Sybil. "No, but her twin sister—my mother—has. Sybil, you're responsible for your sister's death. I hope it haunts you for the rest of your life."

He pulled Sabina's head back and slit her throat from ear to ear. Blood spurted over Imogene, who sat directly in front. Her scream spurred Alistair into action. Sean jumped toward him and Alistair swung the brass candlestick in defense. The ornamental holder pierced the young man's forehead, and he dropped. A stream of blood spurted from the wound.

A moving light appeared at the stair base. Hugh, camera on shoulder, filmed as he entered the chamber. He passed the camera to Susanna and grabbed for Jeremiah.

Imogene stood. "Rahmiel, help us!"

The atmosphere charged as shapes formed. Dark and light figures coalesced and sharpened into distinct otherworldly creatures.

The Light Beings slashed at the demonic entities with their swords, and the smell of sulfur filled the small chamber. In the light of the Light Beings' iridescence, Braeden and the other humans stared as the grotesque dark figures grappled with the angelic ones. The dark creatures reeked of fire and brimstone.

Hugh grabbed his camera from Susanna and panned around the room. Braeden saw Sabina and the young man were both dead and, filled with rage, sprang toward Ezekiel. They struggled, until Ezekiel broke away and ran down a tunnel. The Yates men raced after him, rushing to get away. The dark entities flowed past Braeden, and down the tunnel.

Then there was silence.

Braeden picked up Imogene and held her close, as Xantara helped Sybil stand. Imogene sobbed quietly as her father carried her upstairs. Xantara, Sybil and the media partners emerged at the priest hole entrance.

The church door burst open and black-clad commandos stormed in. They pointed assault rifles at the group, and the commander stepped forward. "Outside, now." The commandos marched them into the car park.

Braeden tried to speak, but a rifle's prod stopped him. The commander walked into the car park. "Names?"

"Doctor Braeden Pembroke, my wife Xantara, Imogene my daughter. Sybil, and... he looked around. "Where's Bryony?"

Hugh and Susanna identified themselves. Hugh tried to hide his camera behind his back. "I saw Jeremiah grab her," he said. "They forced her to go with them."

Braeden set Imogene down, and she leaned against his leg. "The Yates family fled down the tunnels, two people are dead, and Bryony's missing."

The commander signaled his men, and six commandos entered the church.

A tremendous explosion from the church rocked the ground and knocked everybody off their feet. The last two commandos, who had just entered, flew through the air, followed by flames shooting in every direction. A ball of smoke billowed out as the roof exploded. The clock tower collapsed and the leaded windows shattered.

Dazed, Braeden shook his head and stood. He helped others up and stared at the ruined church. Sabina, and now Bryony. The blast must have killed her.

Detective McCullage arrived and sprinted over to them. "What happened?"

Braeden stepped forward. "Ezekiel and Jeremiah were in the tunnels, so they have to be dead. Bryony, too."

The commander ordered Braeden, Xantara, Imogene and Sybil into an armored car. They ushered Hugh and Susanna into another, and swiftly drove away.

Imogene curled into a ball on the seat and cried. "Daddy, they've killed Grannie and Aunty Bryony."

"Sweetie, they've gone to a good place. You've been there. They'll be okay."

Imogene nodded, and Braeden exchanged a glance with his wife.

What next?

Braeden recognized the complex as they drew near Porton Down, a sensitive base for military research. He'd heard the facility developed and tested chemical weapons. Why would they bring them here?

The black-clad commandos ushered them into a low-set building. They must have taken the Channel Five couple elsewhere. Braeden held Imogene's hand and followed his wife and Sybil into a bare room. "Why are we here?"

The commando went out, closed the door, and locked it without a word.

Tears slid down Imogene's face. "I'm sorry, Daddy. This is because of me."

Braeden bent down and clasped her to his chest. "Sweetie, this isn't your fault. I'm sure they'll let us go home soon."

The door opened, and a small thin grey-haired man, with wire spectacles perched on the end of his nose walked in. He held out his hand to Braeden. "Doctor, I'm Professor Ernst Schneider, and I'll be taking care of you and your family. Please follow me."

The professor led them down a series of corridors to an unoccupied hospital ward. Braeden looked around. The large white room held several beds, clinical but apparently comfortable. A central table could seat six, in padded white leather chairs. "There's a well-stocked kitchen through those doors," the professor said. "Please help yourselves."

Braeden caught his arm as he turned to go. "How long do you intend to keep us?"

"Not long. The Prime Minister has asked me to evaluate your daughter. He needs the truth of her mystical incident. I'll require statements from you in due course."

The family sat down, and Xantara turned to Braeden. "Love, look at Imogene."

Braeden turned to study his daughter. She sat on a bed, her eyes wide, nodding as if conversing with an imaginary friend. He waved a hand in front of her face, but she didn't react. After a few moments, her eyes refocused.

"Imogene darling, are you okay?"

"Yes, Rahmiel's here. She said not to worry."

"Does it frighten you when she appears?"

"No, Daddy. I like it. It makes me feel warm and snuggly. Rahmiel's so kind. She would never hurt me."

Sybil went into the kitchen and returned with drinks and sandwiches. "Well, they've stocked up for us. Smoked salmon, no less." She sat and stared at her plate, tears in her eyes. "Poor Sabina. Jeremiah's right, her death is my fault."

Xantara squeezed her shoulder. "Aunt Sybil, his father victimized you, and the blame rests with him. We've all been caught up in these strange events against our will. I ask myself, do we have any control over our lives? I think not."

Imogene spotted a television on the far wall. "Hey—maybe living here won't be so bad."

Ezekiel scrambled into the Land Rover and ordered Obadiah to drive. Jeremiah and Riordan sat in the back seat, with Bryony squeezed between them.

Ezekiel half-turned, and looked at Riordan. "Sorry about your brother. We'll get revenge, you can be sure of that."

Jeremiah smiled at Bryony. "You're a beautiful woman, and today is your lucky day. Yes, a delightful addition to my harem."

The next day Professor Schneider's assistant Nicola came for Imogene, who pulled back. "I want Mommy."

Nicola sighed. "Of course, she may come."

Imogene skipped along the hallway as her mother tried to keep up. "You won't hurt her, will you?" she asked.

"Don't worry, Mom. No one can hurt me. Rahmiel told me so."

Professor Schneider stood as they entered his office. "Thank you, Nicola. Mrs. Pembroke, please wait outside."

Imogene noticed her Mom's stubborn look. "I don't mind, I'll be fine." She pulled her Mother down to kiss her cheek, and watched her leave the room. She looked around. Under the window stood a blond couch with white leather, with no back and one side curled over. She'd seen this type of furniture before, at the IKEA store.

The professor smiled. "So, you like my couch, little one. Would you like to try it out?"

Imogene climbed on, lay down, and looked up at the ceiling. A silver spiral mobile shimmered over her. The man pulled up a chair and sat next to her. He pulled out a crystal on a chain. "Watch this, child. It's pretty, eh?"

Imogene watched the pendulum swing from side to side. Her eyelids became heavy. She might close them for a few minutes.

The professors' voice drifted into her dream. Images of Rahmiel and the Council of Elders floated around her. She found herself in Avebury Circle looking down on the crowd. She spotted her father, but the scene faded. Rahmiel's voice pushed through.

"Nature takes only what it needs. If it takes more, it dies off. Mankind has become greedy. Each individual should let go of self-interest and greed, and share with the under-privileged."

Imogene saw children on the beach, and ran toward them. The sea had receded into the distance, but now it came back, and a huge wave swept them away. She stopped running and stood there, watching. She didn't like it. Those poor children.

The professor's voice grew louder. "I will count down from five to one. When you hear the number one, and I snap my fingers, you will wake up. You will feel happy and relaxed. Five, four, three…"

When Nicola returned from the Ward, the professor grinned. "She's a perfect subject, the best I've ever met. As far as I can tell, she's not lying about the message. In fact, the Rahmiel character spoke again through her, reiterating the need for humanity to change."

"Will you write your report?" Nicola asked.

"Not yet. I need more time with her. She briefly re-lived one of her past lives, and my research into past-life regression cries out for a subject like this. She went under quicker than anyone I've ever known, and I could control her with no problem. I want her back here for another session this afternoon. The opportunity with such a good subject might not cross my path again for years."

Kabshiel waved, and the water stilled. He sat and addressed the gathering.

"In the beginning, love and empathy were the strongest of human instincts. People are connected to each other, and all with the universe. Co-operation is the only way they can survive. Over the years, damaged souls have sent out bad vibrations which have affected other souls. Now the majority want to dominate others and reject democracy, living only for themselves."

The elders nodded, as Kabshiel looked around. "We have given the message, now we will watch and wait. The humans have no conception of the extreme consequences they will set in motion if they ignore our message. The situation is critical."

As Braeden watched Xantara and Sybil teach Imogene to play gin rummy, he realized he'd go stir-crazy if they didn't release them soon. He needed to get back to his patients. How he detested inactivity.

The door opened, and Nicola walked in. "Imogene, the professor would like to see you."

Braeden stepped toward her. "Again? She's a child, for God's sake."

"An hour, at most. She'll be fine."

"I'll go with her this time." Braeden took his daughter's hand and followed the assistant down the hallway.

Nicola paused at the professor's door. "I'm afraid you'll have to wait here. She won't be long." She guided Imogene into the office and closed the door.

Braeden paced the corridor. How did this all start? A happy family, all but destroyed. God, life could be so unfair. Why us?

He heard a soft murmur from the room, and pressed his ear against the door. Damn, he couldn't make out the words. He patrolled the corridor once more. Did Ezekiel and his clan die in the blast? They thought so once before, but the man had nine lives. He hated him, and hated himself for his stupidity. How did that madman suck him in? Would they succeed in setting up more Phineas Priesthood chapters before the authorities tracked them down? Obviously, demonic entities were controlling them.

And why did this mysterious Council of Elders choose Imogene? He couldn't stand to lose her again, and he could guarantee the Priesthood wouldn't give up. Perhaps Porton Down meant safety for his family.

He punched the wall. What was happening in that room? It was his job to protect her, but how can he? He'd let her down before, but he wouldn't do it again.

He settled down to wait for the session to end, and thought about what the future might hold. Will mankind survive?

Following is an excerpt from the second book in the series, 'Imogene's Past Lives'

BONUS – FIRST CHAPTER OF IMOGENE'S PAST LIVES – A THRILLER OF EXTREME CONSEQUENCES

Chapter One

"Doctor Schneider, please stop. I don't want to do it." Imogene watched as he held up the syringe and squirted the liquid. Cold drops fell on her bare arm as she tried to push him away, but he grabbed her, stuck in the needle and pressed the plunger. She clutched the edge of the white leather couch.

"Hush, child. You'll be fine, close your eyes. You are safe here, remember it's just a dream."

Her head swam, and she felt slightly sick. She fought back the waves of darkness, but it was no use. Her fingers relaxed, and she let go.

Kukulcon came for her.

With her arms bound, the young woman stumbled toward the bottomless limestone sinkhole and stared into the pit's black depths as the Shaman pushed her closer. She fought against him, how could this be happening?

The drummers' bright feather headdresses nodded and chanted as they beat the taut leather, and sweat gleamed on their backs in the firelight as they swayed in unison. The girl's heart raced as she struggled. She didn't want to die.

The Shaman gripped her harder and bowed low before the new king. He lifted his spear. "Yum Kaax, God of the Harvest, we offer you this sacrifice. Bless our crops and our people."

He bowed again and dragged her to the edge of the sinkhole. The girl dug in her heels as Kukulcon pushed her. She whipped her foot around his ankle, pulling him off balance, and his primordial scream echoed as they fell together.

Imogene heard Professor Schneider's distant voice.

"Imogene, I'll count down from five to one. At one you will awaken, feeling relaxed and happy. Five, four, three…"

She winced as she opened her eyes. The professor's face was close to hers and she could see her reflection in his wire-rimmed glasses.

"I saw you in my dream, professor. And I saw Ezekiel, the lawyer who murdered me. It was so real it scared me!"

He stood and helped her off the couch. "Don't worry, my child. A bad dream can't hurt you."

Nicola, the professor's assistant, walked her to the waiting room door and opened it. Her father, Doctor Pembroke, rose from his seat.

"We're finished for today," she said. "You may return to the ward."

Dr. Pembroke pushed past them, into the office. "Professor Schneider, I have patients to attend to. When can we go home?"

The professor touched her father's shoulder. "The authorities have the final say, not me. I'll ask the Home Office when I deliver my report."

Imogene clasped her father's hand. "Daddy, let's go back to the ward. Mommy and Aunt Sybil will worry."

Her father took her hand, turned, and without another word led her down the stark corridor.

Inspector Grant studied the Prime Minister and the Home Secretary as they entered his office. The Prime Minister's almost-too-perfect features were marred only by a crescent shaped scar on his forehead. A polo accident, it was rumored, received when he fell and his horse kicked him. His dark hair framed an almost frail complexion, hinting that he suffered from asthma. His ready smile and friendly manner had led to an election landslide. The Home Secretary was an old friend, an ex-royal navy commander he respected and understood. Alex's straight backed stance matched his own.

"This way please."

Inspector Grant looked around Swindon Constabulary's packed incident room, and saw everyone was present. He rapped the table with his pointer.

"Welcome. I'd like to introduce The Prime Minister, Frank Carrington, and Home Secretary, Alexander Brittan. The prime minister wants to be brought up to date on the details of the Stonehenge bombing and massacre. Detective McCullage?"

Jim McCullage stood, loosened his collar and opened the file in front of him. "Sirs, first we had two kidnappings in Swindon, then two shopkeepers went missing in Monkton St Michael. It turns out that Ezekiel Yates, a lawyer and leader of a radical Christian cult, had a mission to rid the West Country of 'sinners'. He kidnapped Xantara Pembroke, wife a Monkton St Michael doctor, because he believed she was a witch."

Frank Carrington held up his hand. "Why did they think that?"

"Well, she and seven other women practice an ancient form of healing. The eldest daughters of eight village families have done this for thousands of years. They call themselves 'The Guardians of Avebury Circle', which is a monument similar to Stonehenge but much older."

"So, what did this Yates man do with her?"

"He locked her in the crypt of a local village church."

McCullage glanced again at his folder as he recounted the events, telling how Xantara's seven-year-old daughter Imogene had earlier been crushed by falling rocks on the Isle of Angels. What was assumed to be an accident turned out to be a murder by Ezekiel Yates.

"He wanted to punish her mother," McCullage said. "He also tried to kill her son, by initiating a car accident. The girl's parents removed her body from the morgue and the Guardians performed a healing ceremony at Avebury Circle."

The room became quiet. The prime minister glanced at the home secretary, then back at McCullage.

"And?"

"And—well, she came back to life, as we all saw on the News Broadcast."

The prime minister slapped his hand on the desk. "That isn't possible. It must have been a trick!"

McCullage took a deep breath. "You haven't heard anything yet," he said, softly. "Here goes. As many people witnessed, the daughter also levitated, and delivered a message from the so-called Council of Elders, right in front of a huge crowd and the world's press."

He kept talking, hoping to get his story out and believed, praying these two important people wouldn't simply walk out. He told about Ezekiel and his followers murdering the two shopkeepers, a young gay lad, and an Indian Sikh in the crypt, and how they dragged Xantara through underground tunnels to the island ruin and tried to burn her at the stake.

"Her husband alerted the pastor and me, and we managed to rescue her," he said.

The Prime Minister frowned. "Well, why didn't you arrest them?"

"They fled back through the tunnels. When lightning struck the tower and collapsed the tunnels, we believed them dead."

Inspector Grant's eyes narrowed. "McCullage, tell him about the underground city."

McCullage knew this was getting weirder and weirder. Would these important visitors just throw up their hands and leave?

"Ezekiel's cousin Obadiah used to be in charge of an underground facility near Corsham, built in the fifties to protect dignitaries from nuclear attack. It was decommissioned years ago, and now he uses it as his personal playground. He kidnapped local 'heretics,' held them prisoner and tortured them to 'convert' them. The group stored explosives in the old armory, and used them to blow up Stonehenge at the summer solstice ceremonies."

He sat down and looked at his hands. Hell, he wouldn't have believed such an outlandish story, either.

Inspector Grant nodded to him and turned to Sam Blackbridge. "We'll now hear from the New York CIA agent, Mr. Blackbridge."

Sam blinked and stood. "Jeremiah Yates, Ezekiel's cousin, bungled a bank robbery in New York and fled to Wiltshire. He heads up the Phineas Priesthood, an even more radical religious cult, whose agenda is to eliminate anyone not Christian and white. We believe he's determined to develop Priesthood chapters in Britain, and the Stonehenge massacre was their first major atrocity to cleanse the country of 'sinners.'"

The prime minister wheezed, then cleared his throat. "Do you believe they're planning another terrorist act?"

"Yes, sir, I do. They are true fanatics, convinced of their own superiority and that they are acting within God's will!"

Frank Carrington turned back to McCullage. "Levitation? Detective, do you seriously believe that?"

Damn. There it was. The whole world saw it, and Carrington asks him if he believed it? "No one knows how she did it," he said. "She ordered the world to abandon its selfish ways, but she spoke with a mature woman's voice, and it wasn't an eight-year-old's speech pattern."

"I thought you said she was seven."

"The day of the speech was her birthday, sir."

Frank stood. "Inspector Grant, what's the status of the terrorists, and where is the girl now?"

"We think the terrorists died in the church explosion after a second attempt to kidnap her. We won't know for sure until we clear the tunnels. Doctor Schneider is evaluating the girl at the Porton Down research facility, as you asked."

Inspector Grant stood stiffly. "Prime Minister, why did you want to keep her at a secret chemical weapon facility?"

"For several reasons. First, it's close to her family home. Second, the complex is secure, and Doctor Schneider is highly qualified. His primary job is to research chemical warfare's psychological effects on the general populace, but he has previous experience with multifaceted childhood issues. He'll use hypnosis and/or drugs to uncover any deceptions."

Ernst Schneider sat at his desk and played the audio of the session he'd just concluded with the Pembroke girl. He called Nicola over. "The child is such a good subject," he said, smiling. "She entered a past life within minutes, and spoke with amazing clarity. I must keep her here, there is so much to learn!"

Nicola sat opposite him, slid her elbows onto the table, and rested her head on her hands. "What happened?"

"She went back to a past life, where she was a human sacrifice to appease a Mayan god. But the remarkable part was that she recognized at least two people from the present day in this past life!"

Nicola frowned. "How could she?"

Schneider tapped his pen against the desk edge as he pondered. "It's collective soul reincarnation," he said, slowly. "The phenomenon is well documented, the most famous case occurred close by in Bath, Avon. A psychiatrist became intrigued when several new patients were plagued with similar bad dreams. The chance of mere coincidence was too great, so he decided to investigate them."

Nicola's eyebrows went up. "What was the collective dream?"

The professor eyed her, unsure of how much to tell her. Finally, he relaxed. "The group experienced being members of the Cathars, a twelfth century religious sect in Southern France. Pope Innocent the Third declared them heretics for their belief in reincarnation, and called for a crusade against them. Thousands were cruelly murdered."

Nicola watched his face closely, as if something troubled her. She leaned back in her chair and crossed her arms. "How did that psychiatrist connect the group?" she asked. "That would seem unlikely."

It was a question he'd asked himself, and researched. The answer was actually quite simple. "He noticed that many of his patients described very similar dreams. After questioning each patient at length, many showed remarkable recall, down to such fixed details as names, family members, and nearby villages. He travelled to France, looked up old records, and dug deep to find the names and locations his patients revealed to him. He couldn't see how such a diverse group could have independently found the information. In any case, they sought help, because the strange dreams disrupted their daily life."

She shook her head. "So, you and I could have experienced past lives together? Do you really believe that?"

"Yes, I believe we could have met before, but relationships might change with each reincarnation. You could be my sister in one life, for example, and my father in another. Each life is designed to work out your Kama. A cruel character in one life becomes the victim next time around. The soul learns their life lesson, or not, then has to repeat the experience."

He paused, thinking. "We have to keep her here until my research is finished," he said, almost to himself.

"How will you arrange that? She has a family, and needs to go to school, lead a normal life."

Schneider formed a steeple with his fingers. "The Prime Minister asked me to evaluate her, and these tests can take a long time. I'll keep her here until I'm sure I have all the information we need. She could reveal new truths to me, and it could prove to be a famous case."

"What about her message and levitation?" Nicola asked. "The authorities will want an explanation for that, it was seen by half the world."

"Of course. I have my methods, and I'll drill into those issues. They mesh nicely into my private research, so I can extend them as long as it takes. Besides, her past lives can connect us with this Council of Elders. I'm convinced they and the Rahmiel personage must live in the spiritual world."

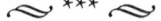

www.ingramcontent.com/pod-product-compliance
Lightning Source LLC
Chambersburg PA
CBHW071311250626
47159CB00004B/1380